THE **SILENCERS**

DONALD HAMILTON

A *MATT HELM* NOVEL

THE *SILENCERS*

TITAN BOOKS

The Silencers
Print edition ISBN: 9780857683397
E-book edition ISBN: 9781781162330

Published by Titan Books
A division of Titan Publishing Group Ltd
144 Southwark Street, London SE1 0UP

First edition: June 2013
1 2 3 4 5 6 7 8 9 10

A CIP catalogue record for this title is available from the British Library.

Printed and bound in the United States.

Did you enjoy this book? We love to hear from our readers.
Please email us at readerfeedback@titanmail.com or write to us at
Reader Feedback at the above address.

To receive advance information, news, competitions, and exclusive
offers online, please sign up for the Titan newsletter on our website:
www.titanbooks.com

THE **SILENCERS**

1

I beat the first real blizzard of the season across the mountains east of Albuquerque, New Mexico. On the high plains beyond, with scattered snowflakes melting on the truck's windshield, I turned south and stopped for lunch in the small town of Carrizozo. The great gray wall of clouds was still chasing me, but here at a lower altitude it could produce nothing but rain.

It was still raining when I had my afternoon coffee and pie in Alamogordo in a joint called the Atomic Cafe. Everything is either nuclear or atomic in Alamogordo; they seem to be very proud of the fact that the first bomb was exploded in their neighborhood. Well, I suppose it's a distinction of sorts, but the bomb I want to see and survive, is the last one.

I asked the man at the cash register what he thought about the underground burst soon to be set off in the Manzanita Mountains, not too far away, now that the Russians had resumed testing. He said it was all right with him. At least he liked it better than an open-air test, with its danger of fall-out if the winds shifted, but he said the folks over in Carlsbad were still worrying about what the shock might do to the great caverns that were their main tourist attraction. He said pretty soon, of course, we wouldn't have these problems. All tests would be conducted in outer space, bothering only the Martians and Venusians. I hadn't heard of that possibility, but then, it's not exactly my field.

"That stuff doesn't bother me," he said. "It's those damn missiles over at White Sands that give me the willies. Did you know that in the early days they'd often go haywire for no reason anybody could figure out and have to be destroyed in the air? They finally realized that local radio transmissions, perfectly legitimate, were taking over control of the guidance systems in some way. Well, suppose the Russkies figured out a way to take over one of the birds and drop it right here in Alamogordo?"

I said, "I thought those things were all rigged so they could be blown up by the range officer pushing a button."

"It doesn't always work, mister," he said. "The Air Force had to shoot one down only last year when it took off on its own and the destruct package failed to function. It was just luck they happened to have a jet in the air with its guns armed when the damn thing came by, or they'd never have caught it…"

It was an interesting conversation, but I didn't have time to continue it. Besides, if I had kept asking questions, he might have thought I was a spy, or that I thought he was. I got back in the truck and kept going.

South of Alamogordo, the highway to El Paso, Texas traverses eighty-four barren miles of sand, mesquite and cactus. It's country that's good for nothing but shooting at, which is just what the government uses it for. It runs from White Sands in the north clear to Fort Bliss in the south, with all kinds of artillery and missile ranges around and between.

All you see from the road are occasional warning signs:

DANGER—PELIGRO
KEEP OUT—NO ENTRE

The Spanish translations remind you that you're nearing the Mexican border.

The sun was shining but low on the horizon when I reached El Paso. I stopped, according to instructions, at the Hotel Paso del Norte, a magnificent relic of the old, bold days when hotels were hotels instead of investments and cattlemen were cattlemen instead of oil magnates. The lobby was at least three stories high and boasted a great blue stained-glass dome supported by pink marble columns. The gentleman who preceded me at the desk wore a big white hat and yellow cowboy boots. His silver belt buckle was the size of a TV screen. I was in Texas.

Waiting, I had the doorman run my old pickup into the parking garage across the street. Then I registered as Mr. and Mrs. Matthew L. Helm, of Santa Rosa, California and explained that my wife would join me later, which was a lie. I'd actually had one, once, but she'd divorced me because she didn't like the kind of work I was doing these days. I couldn't really blame her. Sometimes I didn't like it much myself.

In any event, it seemed unlikely that the management would insist upon proof of matrimony. The instructions I'd received in Albuquerque, while driving east across the country after a job in the high Sierras, had been for me to get down to El Paso right away and register as man and wife, using my own name and giving Santa Rosa as my home town, since there wasn't time to construct a fancy cover for me, and since I'd just been through that redwood country and still had California plates on the truck.

"Do you remember a girl called Sarah?" Mac had asked over the long-distance phone.

"Sure," I'd said. "You mean the one who was working for one of the intelligence outfits in Sweden? Sara Lundgren? A gent on the other team gunned her down in a park in Stockholm."

"Not that one," Mac said. "Sarah with an 'h'. One of our own people. You encountered her in San Antonio, Texas a couple of years ago. There was a misunderstanding about identity, and you got the drop on her and searched her for weapons—quite thoroughly." He cleared his throat. "Very thoroughly indeed, she informed me afterwards, with some heat. I should think you'd recall the incident. She certainly does."

I nodded, forgetting that he could hardly see the gesture—way off in Washington, D.C. "Yes, sir," I said.

"I remember now. A tall girl, not bad looking, in a tailored sort of way. She was going under the name of Mary Jane Chatham at the time, I think. Mrs. Roger Chatham. Her code name didn't figure much in the proceedings, which is why I didn't place her at once."

"Do you remember her well enough to recognize her?"

"I think so," I said. "Brown hair, gray eyes, a good figure, if you like them long and lean, and a trained walk. Said she'd been a model once, and I believed her. Nice long legs. Shy, like a lot of tall girls." I laughed. "Sure, I remember Sarah, the big kid who could blush all over."

"You seem to have the right person in mind," Mac said, "but that last information is not part of her record."

"Make a note of it, then," I said. "She had a thing about taking off her clothes; the only female operative I ever met who'd managed to get through training with her modesty intact. Potentially good stuff, I thought, but a little on the amateur side. What's the matter, has she got herself into something she can't handle?"

"Well, you might say that," Mac said. "She seems to have run into an awkward situation in Juarez, Mexico, just across the river from El Paso. We want to extricate her before any more harm is done. You will therefore…"

He told me what I would do.

"Yes, sir," I said when he'd finished. "Question, sir."

"Yes, Eric?" he said, using my code name formally, almost reprovingly. He likes to think his presentations are complete and no questions are necessary.

"What if she doesn't want to come?" I asked.

He hesitated, and I could hear the singing of miles of wire running across mountains and plains and mountains again clear to the east coast. When he spoke, his voice sounded reluctant.

"There's no reason to think she'll be difficult. I'm sure, when she sees you, she'll cooperate fully."

"Yes, sir," I said. "But not fully enough, apparently, that I can count on her giving me a recognition signal voluntarily. I have to be able to recognize her, you said.

I can't just walk by with a carnation in my buttonhole and wait for her to fall upon me, her rescuer, with delight. It seems odd."

He said coldly, "Don't be too clever, Eric. I have told you all you really need to know."

"I'm sure you're the best judge of that, sir. But you haven't answered my question."

He said, "Very well. I want her back in this country. Get her out."

"How far do I go?" I persisted. He tends to be hard to pin down, when it's a question of giving explicit, unpleasant instructions concerning one of our own people.

I wanted the record perfectly clear. "Do you want her badly enough to take her dead or alive?" I asked.

He hesitated again. Then he said, "Let's hope it won't come to that."

"But if it should?"

I heard him draw a long breath, two thousand miles away. "Get her out," he said. "Goodbye, Eric."

2

My room in El Paso had the kind of spontaneity you get in an old hotel where the bathrooms were added, in any available space, long after the building itself was constructed. I tipped the bellboy, locked the door and sat down to open an envelope with my name on it that had been handed to me at the desk downstairs.

It turned out to contain an official-looking report, ostensibly the fourth and last on this particular job, from an outfit calling itself Private Investigations, Inc. It dealt with the daily activities of a subject calling herself Lila Martinez, now definitely established to be the same person as a certain Mary Jane Helm (Mrs. Matthew L. Helm), born Mary Jane Springer, whom I had asked them to locate. The subject was, it seemed, currently residing in Juarez and working in a place called the Club Chihuahua.

The document ended with the notation that this written report would summarize for my benefit information already submitted by phone. There was also a note to the effect that Private Investigations, Inc. appreciated my patronage and my check, just received. They hoped I had found their work satisfactory, and that I would call upon them again if necessary and recommend them to any of my friends who might be in need of similar discreet assistance. They reminded me that their services were not limited to tracing missing persons, but also included industrial investigations and divorce work. Signed, P. LeBaron, Manager.

I frowned at the report, stuck it back in its envelope and dropped it into my suitcase, making no effort to hide it. In addition to giving me some new background material, it was a prop to establish my character here, if anybody came snooping.

I cleaned up a little, went downstairs, and, rather than get the pickup out of hock, paid sixty cents to have a taxi take me to the international bridge. Two cents let me walk across the Rio Grande into Mexico. The river bed was almost dry. The usual skinny dark kids were playing their usual incomprehensible games around the pools below the bridge.

Stepping off the south end of the span, I was in a foreign country. Mexicans will tell you defensively that Juarez isn't Mexico—that no border town is—but it certainly isn't the United States of America, even though Avenida Juarez, the street just south of the bridge, does bear a certain resemblance to Coney Island.

I brushed off a purveyor of dirty pictures and shills for a couple of dirty movie houses. I side-stepped half a dozen taxi drivers ready to take me anywhere, but preferably to the house of a lady named Maria who had lots of girls, it seemed, one of whom, at least, was the girl I'd been looking for since birth. If I didn't like girls, there were interesting alternatives. I was surprised to learn how many.

But the Matthew L. Helm who'd gone to the trouble and expense of hiring a detective agency to find his missing wife would, I figured, be keeping himself pure for the encounter. I stopped at a bar and had a Margarita cocktail, which is an iced, shaken and strained concoction of tequila, Cointreau and lime juice, served in a glass with a salted rim. You still get a cactus taste from the tequila, which some people can't stand, but I've lived in the southwest long enough, off and on, not to mind a little cactus.

I asked the bartender about places to eat. He said La Cucaracha and La Fiesta nightclubs both served excellent food, with good floor shows, too, but it was too early to go there yet. Nine o'clock—eight o'clock Texas time— was about when the first show came on.

"What about the other places?" I asked. "The ones with real entertainment."

He looked at me reproachfully. "I thought you were asking about food, señor."

I said, "Somebody was telling me about a place called the Club Chihuahua."

"There is such a place," he said. "But you will get no food there. Only liquor and girls. Very bad liquor."

"What about the girls?"

He shrugged. "I will tell you, mister. My advice, if

you want real entertainment—" He glanced around guiltily. "—My advice is, you go to a cat house, if you know what I mean. There, at least, you get real drinks for your money, and you can go to bed with the girls. These other places, they are a big waste of time. They get you all excited, and then what do you do? You still have to find a girl to do it with."

I finally got out of him the fact that the place in which I was interested was up the street from La Fiesta night club, just a block off the street I was on. I walked over that way. With the exception of the nightclub itself, which had a gaudy and impressive front, it was a street of cheap dives, with small knots of shabby, idly talking men blocking the narrow sidewalk here and there. I took a look at the outside of the Club Chihuahua, as dingy as the rest, and got out of there before I succumbed to the temptation of accidentally bumping into a worthy Juarez citizen—hard enough to send him sprawling.

On my way back to the bridge, I stopped to buy my quota of duty-free liquor, one gallon, which I took half in tequila and half in gin. They sell good rum, too, but it's a taste I never acquired. The border whiskey isn't fit to drink. With my armload of bottles, I crossed the river again—it costs one cent going north—and told the man at immigration that I was a U.S. citizen, showed my liquid loot to customs and paid tax on it to the state of Texas, although why Texas should have the right to tax the private liquor of residents of other states has always been a mystery to me.

I came out of the building fairly certain that my activities were a matter of interest to no one—which was what I'd started out to determine in the first place. When I got back to my hotel room, the phone was ringing.

3

I closed the door, parked my load and went over to pick up the jangling instrument

"Mr. Helm?" a hearty male voice asked. "This is Pat LeBaron, of Private Investigations, Incorporated. I just wanted to welcome you to our city and make sure you got our last report all right."

"Thank you, Mr. LeBaron," I said. "The report was waiting for me when I arrived."

"You're lucky to have made El Paso today," he said.

"It looks as if they're in for some weather up in New Mexico and Colorado. We may even get a taste of it here." He paused. "I saw a dove flying south," he said.

"It will return north soon enough," I said, completing the password I'd been given by Mac. That kind of silly, secret-agent stuff always makes me feel self-conscious, and apparently it affected LeBaron the same way, because he was silent for a moment.

Then he said quickly, "Yes, that's very true, isn't it, Mr.

Helm? Spring always comes, if you're around to see it. Is there anything we can do for you while you're in town? I don't want to sound as if I were trying to drum up business, but I thought you might be planning to visit a certain place in Juarez, maybe tonight, and… well, it's not a town you want to wander about alone after dark, if you know what I mean. I feel kind of responsible for bringing you here—"

"How responsible?" I asked.

He laughed. "Well, I'll tell you, we have a set fee for escort work, of course, by the day or hour, but you've been a good client. If you'll just buy me a steak at La Fiesta, I'll go up the street with you afterwards and make sure everything goes okay."

"Well—" I made a show of hesitating.

LeBaron said, quickly and understanding, "Not that I don't think you're perfectly capable of taking care of yourself, haha, Mr. Helm, but I probably know Juarez a little better than you do. I'll pick you up at eight."

At eight on the dot, he called me on the house phone. I took the elevator down to the lobby. A short, sturdy, dark young man got off a sofa and came up to me. For all the width of his shoulders, he had a sleek, patent-leather gigolo look. He had dead-white skin and brown eyes. I'm a transplanted Scandinavian myself, and I have an instinctive mistrust of brown-eyed people, which I admit is perfectly ridiculous.

"Mr. Helm?" he said, holding out his hand. "I'm Pat LeBaron. I'm real pleased to meet you in person, after all the dealings we've had by mail and phone."

I murmured something appropriate, took his hand and gave him the little-finger signal we have, the one that confirms recognition and, at the same time, tells the other guy who's running the show. His eyes narrowed slightly at my immediate assertion of authority, but he gave me the proper response. We stood like that for a moment, taking stock.

No brotherly love flowed between us in that moment. It never does. It's only in the movies that people in the business are partners unto death, linked by iron bonds of friendship and loyalty. In real life, even if your assigned assistant is someone you might like a lot, you damn well don't let yourself. Why bother to get fond of a guy, when you may have to sacrifice him ruthlessly within the hour?

There seems to be a theory among modern business organizations that a man has got to love all his fellow workers in order to cooperate with them. Mac, thank God, has never made this mistake of confusing affection with efficiency. He knows he'd never get a bunch of happy, friendly guys to do the kind of work that we're doing, the way it's got to be done.

He pointed out to me once, in this regard, that the Three Musketeers and their pal D'Artagnan were no doubt a swell bunch of fellows, and that the relationship between them was a beautiful thing, but that when you studied the record you came to the sad conclusion that Louis XIII would have got a lot more for his money, militarily speaking, by hiring four surly swordsmen who wouldn't give each other the time of day.

So I didn't worry when LeBaron and I didn't take to each other on sight. He was a trained man, I was a trained man, and we had a job to do. I could always find some other guy to get drunk with, afterwards.

"The car's out front," he said, releasing my hand. "If you don't mind, we'll walk from the bridge. Things sometimes happen to American cars parked in Juarez at night. It's bad enough leaving it on this side."

"Whatever you say, Mr. LeBaron," I said.

"Hell, call me Pat."

"Pat and Matt," I said, as we went outside. "It sounds like a comedy team."

He laughed heartily. "Hey, that's a good one, Mr. Helm... I mean, Matt. I'll have to remember to tell my wife."

He drove us to the bridge in a blue year-old Chevy sedan and parked it in a lot under one of the long sheds that keeps the sun in summertime from turning your car into an oven. Not that Juarez, or El Paso, either, is much of a place to go in summer. Last July, when I was in Juarez, the temperature was a hundred and twenty in the shade.

We both paid our two cents, crossed the bridge and walked through the carnival atmosphere of Avenida Juarez. The short block to the nightclub was darker, quieter and less reassuring. Going into La Fiesta, we were set upon by taxi drivers who wanted to take us elsewhere, now or later.

"Cab number five," one man kept shouting. "Hey, mister! Cab number five!"

LeBaron nudged me lightly. I glanced surreptitiously

towards the yelling driver, a dark individual with a strong Indian cast to his features. Then we were inside.

Even though I'd been there before, years ago, it was something of a shock, after the gaudy front of the building and the sidewalk hubbub, to be standing suddenly on thick carpeting in a place as hushed and elegant as a good Eastern or European restaurant.

"You saw Jesus?" LeBaron asked softly. He pronounced the name Haysoos, in the Spanish manner. "If we get in a jam, he'll try to bail us out."

"Good enough," I said.

He started to say something else, but the headwaiter came up, bowed and showed us to a small table at the side of the room. LeBaron ordered bourbon whiskey, specifying the brand. I'm always tempted to switch bottles on a guy like that, to see if he can really tell the difference. I ordered a Martini and had another on top of it. No more Margaritas for Mr. Matthew Helm from California. He was no longer in an experimental mood. He was fortifying himself for the ordeal ahead with liberal portions of a known tipple.

As far as I could see, I could have ordered milk or prune juice, and it would have made no difference. Nobody around us showed the slightest interest.

"Is anybody watching this show, do you know?" I asked. "Or are we just performing to an empty theater?"

"We're just doing it for fun," LeBaron said, "unless I've goofed somewhere along the line. In which case we're still just private dick and client."

He had the tough and unreliable look, I thought, of a pool-hall character, and his clothes were flashy enough to point up the resemblance. Well, we can't all look like G-men. He was supposed to be a private investigator, after all, and it's not the most respectable profession in the world.

"How long have you been using this private-eye cover?" I asked.

"Three years," he said. "My wife thinks the government check that comes through once a month is a disability pension from the Veterans' Administration. That's the way it's marked. Well, it's none of her damn business. She's glad enough to get the money and spend it, too."

"Sure."

"Before that, I was in the insurance business in San Francisco. Same deal. Piddle along at a lousy little job until the phone rings and a voice tells you to drop everything… Well, you know how it is."

I nodded, although I didn't really know. I'd never had this kind of long-term standby duty. There had been a war on when I joined the organization, and they broke us in fast. The waiter came up. I ordered steak because that was the safe and conservative thing Mr. Helm from California would order tonight. LeBaron ordered steak, too, but he couldn't just say medium rare, he had to make like a gourmet, describing the exact shade of pink he expected to greet his first exploratory incision with the knife.

Waiting for him to finish briefing the waiter, I watched a couple come in and sit near the dance floor.

The woman was quite pretty, with soft light-brown hair done in one of those big, loose, haystack arrangements currently fashionable. Her gleaming light-blue cocktail dress was cut very simply and fitted very nicely indeed; the little fur jacket she casually shrugged back was of a pale golden color no animal had ever heard of when I was a kid, but they can get a mink to do the damndest things these days.

In contrast to her smart and attractive appearance, the man looked as if he'd dressed for roping cows—boots, stagged pants, checked gingham shirt, suede sports jacket. He was one of those tall, hipless Texas characters who always act as if they'd mislaid a horse somewhere— that is, until you get them out into the back country and show them a real pony with an honest-to-God saddle on it, and it turns out they were never closer to one than in the nearest jeep.

The two of them showed no more interest in us than did anyone else in the place, but something about the woman kept drawing my attention their way. When LeBaron had completed his gustatory arrangements, I gave him the signal, and after a while he turned around casually and looked. He turned back to me and gave the negative sign: he'd never seen her before. Well, that was all right for him, but I'd been something of a photographer once, for a good many years. Faces had been my business, and this one meant something to me, I wasn't quite sure what.

"Not that I'd mind having a piece of it," he said, seeing me still looking that way.

I brought my eyes back where they belonged. "Yeah," I said. "Sure. Not bad at all."

I mean, with a certain type of guy, you've got to pretend to be leching after every woman in sight or he'll think you're not normal. It turned out that my new assistant was one of those who, having once started, could discuss the subject indefinitely. I'd had a long day and several drinks, and I found it hard to keep from yawning. Not that sex itself bores me, you understand, but talking about it just seems like a pointless form of masturbation.

Presently the waiter shut him up by presenting us with our steaks. The orchestra began to play. It was a typical Mexican band, built around a single strident trumpet with power enough to knock you across the room. When Gabriel blows his horn, nobody in Mexico is going to pay any attention—they'll think it's only Pedro or Miguel practicing for the evening's mariachi performance.

A sleek Latin-type male sang a song about his *corazón*. In case you're not up on your Spanish, that's his heart. A very blonde girl in a spangled black dress did some singing, too, as she danced around the floor with the mike, kicking the cord aside when it got in her way. A man in a dinner jacket came out and was funny with a xylophone.

That was it for the floor show. By then it was ten-fifteen and time to go.

4

Outside, we ran the gantlet of taxi drivers and shills and the *porteros* of the various joints we passed who did their best to collar us and haul us into their respective establishments. A tall, gaunt, evil-looking character with a knife-slash across his nose was playing safety man for the Club Chihuahua. We let him make the tackle. It took him less than fifteen seconds to get us seated at a table in a dark room with a bar at one end and a girl undressing on a lighted stage at the other.

The stage was actually a rectangular, slightly raised dance floor surrounded by tables on three sides. At the far end was a curtain, an orchestra, a mike and a master of ceremonies.

"All the way, Corinne!" the M.C. was shouting into the mike. He pronounced the name Coreen. "All the way!" The girl was quite young, quite dark and had a sultry, childish look. Doing a little dance step in time to the music, she dropped her long, confining red dress, constructed so as not to make this operation particularly difficult. Then she did a rudimentary dance with some veils floating from her waistband. Flicking them teasingly at the ringside customers, she disposed of these also. This left her barefoot—she'd already shed her red high-heeled shoes—and in a red satin brassiere and little red satin panties with the approximate coverage of a Bikini bathing suit.

"Jeez, look at that kid!" said LeBaron admiringly. "She can't be a day over sixteen, but jeez!"

I said, "You must have had it tough, keeping an eye on this place."

He glanced at me. "Don't knock it just because you don't dig it, man. So I like to look at girls. It's a crime?" He looked past me. "Uh-oh. Here come the bags."

The portero was ushering a couple of women out of the shadows to sit with us. Mine wasn't too bad—a full-blown dark lady in a short, tight gun-metal gray dress with a little jacket—but LeBaron's prize was swarthy and heavy, not to say fat, with a rough sweater and skirt on that made her look like a female wrestler.

"Hi, boys," LeBaron's girl said. "I am Elena. This is Dolores."

LeBaron performed the introductions from our side. The women sat down, and we ordered drinks which were put on the table almost before we said the word.

"All the way!" the M.C. was shouting. "Take it off! All the way, Corinne!"

The girl was still dancing barefoot around the stage—if you could call it dancing. She was a well-built kid,

I had to admit, and she seemed to be enjoying herself, which was nice.

My lady, Dolores, stroking the back of my neck affectionately, was watching the show. "She is *India*— Indian. You do not have to hurry with your drink, honee. I will not hurry with mine. You will see. This is a friendly place, not a robbery like some of those others."

The dusky young girl on the stage unhooked her red brassiere, snatched it off and ducked behind the curtains, waving it and laughing.

"A child," Dolores said scornfully. "She cannot dance; she cannot sing; all she can do is walk around and take off the clothes. When I was of that age—"

"Where are you from, Dolores?" I asked.

"Chihuahua City, but there is no money there. Here I can still make thirty-five cents a drink. It is a living…"

Busy making conversation, I'd missed the M.C. introducing the next performer. I'd been listening for the name, of course, but he threw me off momentarily by pronouncing it Leela in the Spanish way. Suddenly she was there, the curtains stirring behind her then becoming still.

After the solidly built young Indian girl who'd preceded her, she looked seven feet tall. She wore a yellow satin dress that left her shoulders bare but encased her smoothly from breasts to knees, flaring below to give her a little room to move. Her hair had been dyed black since I'd last seen her. It made her look harder and older than I remembered her.

"All the way, Lila!" the M.C. shouted. "Take it off! All the way!"

She saw us at once, even though our table was at the back of the floor, and almost broke step. I saw the quick apprehension in her eyes. She might not recognize LeBaron, if he'd been careful, but she'd seen me before, and she'd know I wasn't here with help just to take in her act.

I saw her recognize me, and I saw her remember the time I'd made her remove her clothes in a different place, for a different purpose, embarrassing her terribly. A funny little rueful look came to her face at the memory; she might have been regretting a lost innocence. Then she was at the corner, making her turn gracefully along the edge of the floor, using that trained walk I'd noticed— the walk of a high-fashion model, just a little exaggerated and done in time to the music. It was funny to see it in a dive like this.

"Jeez," LeBaron said loudly, "that's a lot of mouse, man. There's six feet of her, if there's an inch." His elbow nudged me. "Identification okay?" he whispered.

"Okay."

"I wasn't quite sure," he whispered, "from the pix. She was the right height and all that, in the right place, but I wasn't, you know, positive with that hair, and I wasn't supposed to risk trying for fingerprints or anything. Washington said you'd confirm. We don't want to get the wrong one. Jeez, that would be something, wouldn't it? Hauling a kicking, spitting Mex dancer across the international border!" He laughed at the thought then and stopped. "Okay, so all we have to do is wrap her up and take her home. The loving husband claiming his errant wife; get ready to make with the dialogue. She'll come out and mingle with the customers as soon as she's finished her act—that is, unless she panics and beats it."

"Do we have any orders in that case?"

"Jesus will try to pick her up outside and see where she comes to rest." He nudged again. "Behind you, when you get the chance. Company… What is it, Elena?"

The fat woman jerked her head towards the tall slender girl on the stage. "Americano," she said scornfully. "No *tetas*. American women have no tetas."

"Tetas?" I said, puzzled. Mr. Helm from California wouldn't speak much Spanish. "What's that?"

Fat Elena jerked up her sweater and showed me what it was. LeBaron laughed heartily.

"Tetas," he said. "You know, like tits. Cover them up, baby…"

He touched me again with his elbow to remind me, and after a moment I looked around casually. There were tall Mr. Texas with his high-heeled boots and his pretty companion with her mutation minks and haystack hairdo. It seems like a hell of a place to bring your girl friend, was my first thought. But what could you expect from a guy who'd take a girl out to dinner dressed for a rodeo?

The woman was watching the stage with stiff fascination. I looked that way again. Sarah, Lila—or was it Mary Jane?—had made her circuit once. Coming back towards us, along the edge of the floor, with an undulating, rhythmic walk, she looked suddenly very young despite her height and the dyed hair and the sexy satin dress—tall and young and kind of scared—but she did not falter. She swung a hip towards a table full of Mexicans and slipped past smoothly, laughing, before they could touch her. She reached out and rumpled the hair of an American tourist, retrieving her hand gracefully before he could seize it.

"All the way, Lila!" somebody shouted from the back of the room.

She smiled. The bloodhounds might be on her trail, but she was going to do her stuff regardless. The kid had guts. Well, I knew that. She'd tried to jump me, the time we'd got our identities confused in San Antonio. I'd been holding two guns at the time, like Wild Bill Hickok, but she'd jumped me anyway.

"All the way!" the M.C. yelled, and the loud-speakers threw his voice at us from the dark recesses of the room. "All the way, baybee!"

She made her corner and passed across the front of the stage, swinging away from us. Her back turned toward us, she reached up and did something feminine and provocative with her hair, teasing, before she reached for the zipper. As the yellow dress opened from top to bottom, baring her back, a knife, coming from nowhere, buried itself to the hilt just below her left shoulder blade.

5

I made no apologies for letting it happen. My job wasn't to protect her life, it was to get her out of an awkward situation alive or dead. I'd made sure that my instructions were quite clear on that point. If I'd been sent to preserve her from bodily harm, I'd have run the whole thing differently, and Mac would undoubtedly have worded his orders differently.

I heard two quick warning whistles, barely audible, from LeBaron, meaning watch at your right (three means on your left and one means behind you), but I'd been in this business longer than he, and I'd already taken care of Dolores. Maybe she was just a nice friendly girl from Chihuahua City, but she'd been planted on us by the management and I wasn't taking any chances. She folded when I clipped her, and I laid her head gently on the table, tucked a five-dollar bill into the front of her dress by way of apology and looked around.

It was a nice hellish scene by this time. The long, dark

room was in a turmoil as everybody tried to make it out the door before the police arrived. There were curses in Spanish, English and Texan. Meanwhile, on the brightly lighted stage at the other end, forgotten, the tall girl had gone to her knees in agony, feeling in back for the thing that hurt her. She couldn't quite reach it, and she fell forward onto her yellow-satin stripper's dress, spread out as if to receive her.

LeBaron had muffed it. Fat Elena knew judo, too, apparently, and she was giving him a hard time. I couldn't be bothered with them. I started for the stage, and somebody running past knocked me off balance. I caught a whiff of expensive perfume and felt soft fur brush against me.

"Janie!" a woman's voice gasped. "Oh, Janie…!"

I picked myself out of the chairs and tables, and made it up to the stage. The lady of the minks was ahead of me, but the M.C. was ahead of her, crouching over the fallen girl. She tried to pull him away so she could get in there, and he drove an elbow back and knocked her down. It was my turn, and I got him to his feet with a heave. He didn't weight much, just a little white-faced, black-mustached runt in a loose-fitting dinner jacket.

He spun to face me, snarling, and reached under his shiny lapel. I did something flashy with my hands, and as he prepared to duck or parry the blow, I kicked him hard in the groin. He doubled up and fell down, moaning. I heard the one-whistle signal for danger behind and dropped on top of him. Something went over me. I rolled aside to see the tall, scarred portero raising a blackjack for another blow, but LeBaron was in back of him now. LeBaron dropped him with a chop to the neck.

I glanced at mine while LeBaron made sure of his. Mine was nothing to worry about. They weren't going to straighten him out in less than half an hour with anything less than a block and tackle. LeBaron's was his business and I left it to him. I heard the thud of a kick as LeBaron made sure we weren't bothered for a reasonable length of time. I was already turning back to the girl on the floor.

The pretty lady of the furs was kneeling beside her. When I saw the two faces close together and the similarity of the bone structure, I knew, of course, what had caught my eye in the nightclub down the street. The girl opened her eyes.

"Gail!" she breathed.

The kneeling woman touched her cheek with a gloved hand, hesitantly, the way you touch the dying. "Don't talk, dear. I'm sorry for everything, Janie. We'll get you home where you belong…"

The girl shook her head, almost imperceptibly. She licked her lips and spoke with difficulty: "Under my hair, in back… Here. Take it." Summoning all her strength, she reached for something at the nape of her neck, pulled it loose and passed it over. Her eyes looked up and found me. I thought I saw a sort of challenge through the film of pain. "Gail," she breathed, "bend closer, listen, it's important, the whole world… the whole world."

Then she was whispering inaudibly, as far as I was concerned, in the older girl's ear. A moment later she was dead. Gail looked up at me quickly, shocked and unbelieving.

"She's dead!"

"Yes."

"But she's my sister. My little sister! When I heard she was working in this awful place, I came all the way from—"

"Sure," I said. "Come on."

"We can't leave her like this!"

"She'll be taken care of. Come on."

I glanced at LeBaron, standing guard. He jerked his head towards the rear. He was mopping his cheek with a bloodstained handkerchief. The portero hadn't touched him, but Elena had got in at least one good lick with her fingernails. I looked around. The place was still bedlam, but our particular part of it wasn't popular. This was Juarez, where you didn't associate with dead bodies if you could possibly help it—you went elsewhere fast. LeBaron put his handkerchief away and looked down.

"What about it?" he asked. "The man in Washington said get her out."

I'd had a decision to make, but I'd already made it. It was a neat disciplinary point—there are certainly times when orders should be followed to the letter—but there are also times when a little judgment is advisable. I didn't think Mac really had any use for a dead girl, particularly when there was a live one handy.

"She's out," I said. "Whatever she had, she just passed it. Let's go… Come on, Gail."

Sarah's sister—or Lila's or Mary Jane's—was still kneeling there, numb and dazed. "But Sam, the man I was with—"

"The hell with Sam," I said. "Have you ever seen the inside of a Mexican jail, honey?"

Even in that moment, in that place, she didn't like being called honey. I was presuming on too short an acquaintance. I could see that we could spend all night there getting introduced properly, so I picked up her little white purse from the floor where she'd dropped it. I shoved it into my pocket and gestured to LeBaron. He got one arm and I got the other, and we set Gail on her pretty little blue high-heeled shoes and marched her towards the curtains at the rear of the stage.

"Left and out," LeBaron said. "Jesus had better have the cab waiting, damn his black Yaqui soul." After a moment, he said, "The portero threw the knife. I should have kicked him harder. I'm afraid he'll live."

"The M.C. was in it, too," I said. "He was searching the girl for something when we interrupted him."

"Searching? She didn't have much to search, just a bra and G-string."

"She had it in her hair, whatever it was. She got it from that American tourist, I think. I never saw his face, but she patted his black hair nicely as she went by, and he reached up to grab her, remember?" I glanced back and said, sentimentally and uselessly, "Poor kid."

"Yeah."

This wasn't all just idle chitchat, you understand.

We were pooling what information we had, while we had the chance, in accordance with standard operating procedure in case only one of us got out to make a report. The woman between us tried to pull free and gasped with pain as we both clamped down—the cops used come-alongs made of chain and stuff, nicely chrome plated, but there are perfectly good grips that serve the same purpose.

"Let me go!" she protested. "Let me go!"

LeBaron was leading, since he knew the way. I was keeping an eye out behind us, so I was the first to see the Texas cavalry come charging to the rescue as we reached the curtains. Somebody had clobbered him good in the melee, but not good enough, and he stumbled up to the stage in his silly boots, with his face streaming blood from a cut over the eye.

"You there!" he yelled. "Get your cotton-picking hands off that lady, you sons of bitches!"

Then, so help me, he pulled a gun. In a place like that, with hell breaking loose already, he pulled a gun. A guy like that would light a cigar in a fireworks factory.

I shouted, using the name the woman had mentioned: "This way, Sam! Make it snappy! We've been waiting for you!"

It didn't work. The invitation didn't register. We were strangers; we were hostile; we were manhandling his girl, and you can't do that to a Texan, suh. He took another step and stood there swaying, waiting for the weapon in his hand to settle down on something so he could shoot it.

"Left and out," LeBaron said quickly, urging us through the curtains. "Jesus will get you across the river. Never mind the cowboy, I'll take care of him."

He started back across the stage. I didn't wait to see what happened, but I heard a shot as I pulled the reluctant woman through the narrow passage and out through a door that stood open as if we weren't the first to escape that way.

I waited just a moment outside, but LeBaron didn't come. Maybe I'd see him again and maybe I wouldn't. Like I said, trained men doing a job. You don't have to love each other like brothers, but the next time, if there was a next time, he could talk about sex all he wanted, even if he had been a little slow in dealing with Elena…

"Cab number five!" a voice called softly.

We were in an alley of sorts. It was seemingly empty, the way certain parts of certain towns get when there's trouble, but you could feel eyes watching from all the shadows. I headed towards the voice. A man showed himself briefly, beckoning. I ran after him through the narrow space between two buildings, dragging Gail along with a grip that wouldn't let her resist without tearing some ligaments.

The parked cab on the street beyond was battered and ancient, but it looked remarkably like the promised land at that moment. I shoved my companion into the back and piled in after her. Jesus had the heap moving before I got the door closed.

A minute later we were on a street full of lights and

people. It was hard to believe that there were still places in Juarez where tourists haggled innocently over so-called Swiss watches and native ponchos. Jesus turned off this street, driving circumspectly, and made some more turns that left me lost.

"There is the bridge, señor," Jesus said presently without turning his head. "I do not think they will stop us on this side, there has not been sufficient time for an alarm, but on the other side there will be the usual questions. The lady is a citizen of the Estados Unidos?"

"Yes. At least I think so."

"She must say it, señor. Remember that. They will ask and wait for the answer. They will act as if it is not important, but the words must be spoken, always."

"Thanks, Jesus."

It was nice to work with bright people. He had noticed that the third occupant of the cab wasn't really happy in my company. I glanced at Gail. She was rubbing her strained wrist. In the darkness of the cab, she did not look noticeably disheveled in spite of what she'd been through. Her fluffy, tumbled hairdo was only a little more so, her dress and furs and gloves seemed to be intact, and if all went well nobody was going to examine her shoes and stockings, so I didn't. But I did note that she had a tense, wound-up look that said she was only waiting for a chance to make trouble.

I took a ball-point pen out of my pocket without letting her see it. I couldn't risk being separated from her by chivalrous immigration inspectors, even briefly. Right then, I couldn't afford to let her out of my sight for a moment. I took her in my arms, rammed the pen into her side, and spoke softly in her ear.

"It's a gun, Gail," I said. "We don't want trouble. But if there is trouble, honey, you'll sure as hell get it first."

She didn't move or speak. I saw the bridge loom before us, and I laid myself against her and kissed her hard, holding the pen in her ribs. I claim no credit for originating the idea. It's been done before, in the movies and elsewhere. The thing about it is that it often works. The cab stopped. Money changed hands as Jesus paid the toll. There were sympathetic words in Spanish, and appreciative laughter. The cab drove on.

"We have passed the Mexican side," Jesus reported. "No sweat, si?"

My companion smelled nice, and she felt warm and feminine, but it wasn't really much of a kiss. There was a noticeable lack of enthusiastic cooperation, and I felt considerably like a fool, slobbering over the face of a woman whose main reaction was probably a strong desire to throw up. The cab stopped again, and somebody asked a question. I came up for air and saw a face surmounted by a uniform cap at the window.

"Oh," I said foolishly. "What was that, officer?"

"Did you buy anything in Mexico, sir?"

"Not this trip," I said.

"What is your citizenship?"

"U.S.," I said.

"And yours, ma'am?"

The woman in my arms hesitated. I nudged her with the pen. She drew a long breath.

"I'm American," she said.

The uniformed character straightened up, stepped back and waved us on.

I said, "Honey, you shouldn't have said it like that." She glanced at me quickly, startled. "But—"

"Our neighbors don't like it," I said. We were driving away, but it seemed best to be heard talking naturally. "They're not our continents, you know, either one of them, although sometimes we act as if we own them both. Jesus is American, too, aren't you, Jesus?"

"Si, señor."

"You, Gail, are a citizen of the United States of America," I went on pedantically, "but from Hudson's Bay to Tierra del Fuego we're all Americans together… It's the Hotel Paso del Norte, Jesus."

"Si, señor."

A few minutes later, I was ushering Gail into my sixth-floor room at the hotel. I locked the door behind us, and took my hand out of the pocket, leaving the ball-point pen there. I looked at the pretty, slightly rumpled woman standing in the center of the room.

"Now, Gail," I said gently, "you'd better give me what your sister gave you, and you'd better tell me what she told you, word for word."

6

After a moment, she laughed. Then, deliberately, she turned away from me and walked across the room to the dresser, studying her reflection in the mirror. She pulled up her long white kid gloves, grimaced at a smudged palm and tried to rub it clean. She smoothed down and brushed off her dress. The gleaming blue stuff was brocade, I noticed. My grandmother upholstered her sofa with it, but nowadays they wear it.

"May I have my purse, please?" she asked.

"No."

She glanced at me sharply, and swung back to face me, settling the fur jacket about her shoulders.

"My dear man, let's stop this foolishness. You haven't really got a gun in your pocket, have you?"

It was my first opportunity to study her at leisure at close range in good light. She was a very attractive woman, slender and graceful, slightly above average height, but, unlike her sister, not conspicuously so. I've been calling her pretty, but there was more than prettiness in her face. She had very large, clear gray-blue eyes, skillfully accentuated by make-up. She had a slim, aristocratic nose. She had fine cheekbones, with that faint, delicately haggard hollowness below that the girls all try for...

I mean, she was almost perfect, but the mouth gave her away. Not that it wasn't fundamentally a generous and well-shaped mouth, even if the lipstick had suffered some recent damage. It was a mouth with good potentials, but you could tell she'd never taken advantage of it. She'd never had to. She'd undoubtedly got by on her looks since she was a baby, and now, at thirty give or take a year or two, her mouth had the betraying, calculating, spoiled and selfish expression characteristic of the professional beauty.

There was the mouth to give her away, and there was the business of my alleged weapon. She hadn't had the guts to call my bluff at the bridge, as her sister would have done. This wasn't a woman who'd ever charge the muzzle of a loaded revolver, for any cause. No, she'd waited until it was perfectly safe to act brave and scornful.

I took the pen out of my side pocket, showed it to her without comment and clipped it to my inside pocket where it belonged. I got her purse out and looked inside it. Her various identity cards couldn't seem to agree on her last name, but I gathered she'd been born Gail Springer and lived in Midland, Texas. I remembered that the name Mary Jane Springer had figured in Pat LeBaron's report. I tucked the little wallet back into the purse and looked up.

"If you're looking for something respectable to call

me," she said, "Mrs. Hendricks will do. He was the last, and I guess I'm still entitled to use his name."

"The last?" I said.

"The last for the time being, anyway," she said. "Before that, I was Countess von Bohm for a little while, and then there was that polo player from Argentina, and before that there was a cowboy named Hank, my only true love. I ran away with him when I was seventeen, and he broke his neck in a rodeo a month later."

"Tough," I said.

She moved her shoulders beneath the furs. "So? He only had one neck, and Daddy would have broken it for him, anyway, when he caught up with us. Or, we'd have got on each others' nerves or something. This way I can remember how it was, bright and beautiful and unspoiled."

She said it all with a perfectly straight face, but she was kidding somebody in a bitter sort of way, me, herself, or a boy named Hank who'd died to give her a pleasant memory.

I asked, "How's Sam on horseback?"

"Sam?" She laughed. "What makes you think that phony can ride, those forty-dollar boots?"

"That's about the way I had him figured," I said. "What's his full name?"

"Sam Gunther." She drew a breath to indicate that her patience was at an end. "If you won't let me have my purse, at least give me my comb and compact and lipstick. I'd like to go into the bathroom and wash my face, for obvious reasons."

"No bathroom," I said.

"My dear man—"

"My dear woman," I said, "you stay where I can watch you until you give me what I want. Unfortunately, I didn't see you hide it. There were other things of more compelling and immediate interest to observe."

She said with sudden harshness: "Damn you! She was my sister! Don't talk as if her death was just a cheap act for your entertainment."

I shook my head. "I'm sorry. I didn't mean it that way, believe me. I knew her too, slightly." I hesitated, but whether I liked Mrs. Gail Hendricks or not, she seemed to be genuine, and I had to give her the break of telling her a certain amount of truth. I said, "I went to that place to meet her. She worked for us, you know."

The big, beautiful grayish eyes narrowed. "Worked for... What are you, a strippers' agent or just a pimp?"

I said, "You're selling your sister short, Gail. I'm an agent, all right, but not that kind. And she was an agent, too. Did you think she was working in that joint for fun?"

"No," she said, "I thought—"

"What?"

She sighed. "Well, what would you think if your kid sister ran away from home in a... well, let's call it a highly disturbed state of mind, and when you heard of her again, after several years, she'd dyed her hair and was stripping in a Juarez dive?"

I said, "You thought she'd just hit the skids, is that it?"

"What else could I think? When some friends—

friends!—told me, with that ghoulish kind of sympathy, enjoying every minute of it, that they'd just been to Juarez and there was something I ought to know but they didn't know quite how to tell me… Well, I couldn't go alone, not into a joint like that, so I got hold of Sam, and we drove down together. He didn't want to go, but I told him he owed her that much, we both did."

"Owed her?" I said.

Gail moved her shoulders slightly. "A pretty little family triangle. You know, the attractive older sister—if I may flatter myself a bit—and the big horse of a younger sister, awkward and shy, and the tall, handsome young man. Sam was just doing it for kicks, or maybe he had an eye on her money—we both got quite a bit when Daddy died—but she was desperately in love with him. To her, he was the first man to see the true beauty of her soul underlying the gawky…" She stopped abruptly. "That was bitchy, I guess. She's dead. I didn't mean to make fun of her. Strike it from the record, please."

I said, "So you took him away from her. To save her?"

She shrugged again. "Thank you, sir. I'm sure my motives were lovely, perfectly lovely. They always are. Anyway, she caught us and… well, never mind the details. I'll admit she scared me silly. I thought she was going to kill us both. She had a gun, and she'd always been good with horses and firearms and fishing rods and things. But she just threw the damn gun out the window. In the morning she was gone. I tried to find her, and I did catch up with her once, in New York, where she was doing some modeling, but she slammed the door in my face. After that, I let it go. If that was the way she wanted it…" Gail gave that little shrug again. "The next time I heard, several years later, she was in Juarez. The rest you know." She looked at me steadily. "If you're a government agent of some kind—I suppose that's what you're hinting at—show me something to prove it."

I said, "We don't carry badges. They have a habit of cropping up at inconvenient moments."

"I'm supposed to take your word for it?"

"It would make things easier on both of us," I said.

"I don't doubt it would make things easier for you!" she said scornfully. "But you're forgetting one thing, aren't you? I was there. I saw it. Mary Jane didn't want to give you anything. She didn't want to tell you anything. You were standing right over us, and she looked you straight in the eye and turned to me. How do you explain that, Mister So-called Agent?"

"I don't explain it," I said. "I don't have to."

She frowned. "What do you mean?"

I said, "When we have finished in this room, please remember that I told you the truth from the very start. I told you that I am an agent of the U.S. Government. I asked you to turn over to me certain property and information given you by your sister, a member of the same undercover organization as myself. These are facts. I probably shouldn't have revealed them to you, and I may even catch hell for doing it, but I'm putting my cards on the table and asking you nicely—"

She said, "My dear man, if you expect me to believe you without any evidence whatever, you must think me an awful fool!"

"Oh, I do," I said gently. "I think you're the sophisticated kind of fool who'd rather play safe and assume all men are liars than risk trusting one and maybe have him make a sap out of you. But I had to give you a chance, if only for your sister's sake."

She said angrily, "Why in heaven's name should I trust you, a man I've never seen before! A man who ran out and left his friend in the lurch!"

"Don't talk about things you know nothing about, Gail," I said. "When two men on the same team are running down a field, and one is carrying a football, does he lay down the ball when trouble occurs and go back to help his poor outnumbered teammate, or does he keep plugging for the goal?"

"It's not quite the same thing! This is… I don't know what it is, but it certainly isn't a game!"

"No, and you're not a football, either. But the principle remains." I looked around for something you find in most hotel rooms. It wasn't in plain sight, but I found it in a dresser drawer—a Gideon Bible. I placed my hand upon it and looked the woman in the eye. "What I have told you is the truth, the whole truth, and nothing but the truth, so help me God."

I put the Bible away. There was a little silence; then Gail shook her head quickly. It was corn and she was no goose; she wasn't going to swallow it.

"Mary Jane obviously didn't want you to have it," she said. "I can't just take your word. If you had *something* to prove—"

I said, "It would take me anywhere from a couple of hours to a day or two to get proof here that would satisfy you. That's too long to sit in this room watching to make sure you don't do something clever with what you're carrying, or just something perverse to spite me. We'd both get pretty damn tired of it, not to mention such details as eating, sleeping, and going to the john. I'll tell you this. Mary Jane's feeling against me was probably personal. We got at cross purposes once, we got our signals mixed…" I told her about the incident in San Antonio. "That was before she was assigned a job that involved undressing in public and got over being embarrassed by the idea. I know of no other reason why she should have acted the way she did tonight."

That was still the truth, if only just barely. I didn't know of a reason, even though Mac's attitude had indicated there might be one.

Gail hesitated, watching me. "What were you and Janie doing in San Antonio?"

I said, "That comes under the heading of classified information."

"What branch of the government do you work for?"

"Same answer."

She said, "If you're really a government man, why did you have to smuggle me through immigration, with a pretend gun in my ribs?"

I said, "For one thing, I was afraid they might separate us before I got my story told and confirmed; I didn't want to let you out of my sight. For another thing, my chief doesn't like us letting other government agencies into the act when it isn't absolutely necessary." I paused, and went on: "Gail, I've already told you more than I should. There are a million questions you could ask, most of which I couldn't answer, either because I don't know the answer or because I'm not free to give it. And at the end of it, you'd still have to look at me and decide whether I was lying or telling the truth. So let's not waste the time. Make up your mind. Are you going to trust me or aren't you?"

I saw at once that I'd overdone it. The word "trust" killed it. You can use it once, kind of diffidently, but essentially it's a dirty, conniving, treacherous, sneaking word these days. If you ask somebody to trust you, twice, he knows you're playing him for a sucker—if he's smart, and she was smart. Nobody was going to put one over on her.

"No!" she said.

I drew a long breath. "Well, in that case... It seems that every time I meet one of the Springer girls, I have to ask her to take her clothes off."

She stared at me, shocked. "My dear man—"

I took a step forward. "As they said in that place: all the way, Gail. All the way."

She took a step backwards and wound up against the dresser. She drew herself up in a dignified way. "Really—"

I said, "You're being pretty silly. You're not Mary

Jane. You can't possibly be embarrassed, not a woman who's had four husbands and a Sam Gunther, at the very least. Incidentally, if you try to scream or go for the phone or anything like that, you'll wind up sitting on the floor with all the wind knocked out of you."

She said angrily, "You wouldn't dare! If you think you can bluff me again—"

There was that, of course. I was starting from behind; I'd already bluffed her once, with a ball-point pen, and it rankled. She wasn't going to fall for my tough-guy act again. She knew that behind my crusty exterior lurked a marshmallow heart.

If it had only been a matter of searching her, I might still have tried to work it our peacefully, but she not only had to be made to give me something, she had to be made to tell me something. I had to impress her, somehow, with my fundamentally vicious nature. Now she was talking again, in her haughty and indignant way, and her attitude gave me a pain, anyway. I just reached out and yanked the dress off her.

7

It didn't come off quite as easily as that, of course. It wasn't a movie break-away garment or a stripper's dress with a smooth-working full-length zipper. It was a smart and expensive and well-constructed cocktail dress of strong material—as I said, my grandmother used that shiny figured stuff for upholstery purposes—so I had to get a good grip and pull down quite hard, twice, slantingly right and left, just to break it loose from her shoulders and out from under her furs.

She took a moment to realize what was happening; then she grabbed for the dress as it tore away, and we had a breathless and undignified struggle over the garment before I captured her wrists and got them into my left hand. With my right, I got another grip on the slick, heavy brocade, which had slipped to her waist as we wrestled. Holding her by the wrists, I gave a long, slashing, sideways jerk that ripped open the seam down the side. A final tug burst it apart at the hem, and I had it all.

I stepped back, releasing her. She started after me instinctively, reaching out, but checked herself, realizing, I guess, that even if she could get it back, the crumpled rag I was holding wouldn't do her much good.

We faced each other like that. She looked kind of silly standing there in her furs, her long white gloves, her blue high-heeled pumps—plus brassiere, pantie-girdle and stockings. She looked like one of those leggy pinups, you see in bars and garages, that are always getting their skirts snagged on barbed-wire fences in interesting ways. But she wasn't quite as young as those models. Not that there was anything aged about her face and figure. She just wasn't a laughing, teasing kid, that's all. She was a grown woman, humiliated and furious.

I said, "All the way, Gail."

She started to speak and couldn't; she was too angry. And the terrible thing is there was nothing she could do about it, dressed as she now was, that wouldn't look perfectly ridiculous and at the same time rather provocative. She had the sense to know it, and she drew a long, uneven breath, and forced a rueful smile with all the warmth and sincerity of a Borgia kiss.

"Well!" she breathed. "A man of direct action!"

"I gave you a chance," I said. "I gave you every chance in the world. You wouldn't believe me, not even with the Bible thrown in. Now I ask you again, do you give me what I'm looking for or do I have to strip you completely to get it?"

She glanced down and grimaced. "Damn you.

That dress cost me a hundred and seventy-five dollars last week in Dallas. I'd never worn it before." After a moment, she said wryly, "Well, I can't see much point in putting up a losing battle for my girdle and bra. Here." She reached two fingers inside her brassiere, pulled something out and gave it to me. I took it and found it to be a small metal cylinder wrapped in something sticky, like double-faced Scotch tape. That would make it easy to hide, under the hair or elsewhere; it would stay put. Inside the cylinder was a tight roll of microfilm. I don't know how the undercover professions got along before the stuff was invented.

I glanced up briefly. Gail had peeled off her long gloves and was removing her mink jacket, which was smart if not modest. A fashionable lady, gloved and furred for the street, who suddenly misplaces her dress, is a rather comical sight, but there's nothing funny about a beautiful woman in stockings and undergarments. It can be irresistible, or it can be merely embarrassing, but it isn't funny. She came to stand beside me—now deliberately unself-conscious about her half-clad state—and took cigarettes and a lighter from her purse on the dresser. I didn't stop her.

"What is it?" she asked.

I had pried the microfilm out of its tiny cartridge. There were only five exposures on the strip, and it had been rolled so tightly it was difficult to handle. I could barely make out the letterhead on the first frame. The rest of the printing was much too tiny to decipher with the naked eye. I rolled up the strip, returned it to the cartridge and put it in my pocket.

"Well?" she said,

I shook my head. "It's none of your business, certainly, and maybe none of mine. Anyway, I can't read it without a viewer." This wasn't quite true. As an ex-photographer, I travel with a bunch of camera junk among which is an achromatic seven-power magnifier that would have done the job after a fashion, but at the moment I had more important matters to concern me. "Now give me the rest of it," I said.

She smiled slowly, lit the cigarette she had placed between her lips and blew smoke at me. She was a beautiful woman without too many clothes on, and she knew it.

"Make me," she said.

I said wearily, "Gail, you never learn, do you?"

Her eyes narrowed slightly. "What do you mean?"

I said, "Haven't you got it through your pretty head yet that I'm going to get that information from you, one way or another?"

"It sounds—" She blew more smoke at me. "—it sounds as if you were planning to torture me. How quaint!"

I said, "Don't talk about torture as if you know what it meant. You haven't the slightest idea."

She smiled slowly. "Then tell me."

I'd shaken her for a moment, or my violence had, but she'd recovered fast. Losing a dress was, after all, not really a tragedy. She'd undoubtedly had several nice dresses torn or hopelessly mussed in her life—I judged it had been that kind of a life—and she'd made a man pay for every one of them. She was going to try to make me pay for this one, sooner or later. In the meantime, she was going to make me as uncomfortable as possible, lounging there sexily with a cigarette between her fingers.

"Tell me," she murmured. "Tell me about torture, darling."

"Very well," I said. "There are two forms. One is long and sure. It consists of breaking the subject's will to resist by inflicting severe pain and physical injury—but not fatally—over extended periods of time, combined with other forms of humiliation and hardship that add to the psychological effect. No one is immune to this. During the war, for instance, many brave and dedicated underground workers betrayed their comrades after being in the hands of the Gestapo for a while. This was expected, and operations were therefore conducted by small units, the other members of which fled to safety as a matter of course the minute one person was captured."

She put the cigarette to her lips. "Go on, Professor."

I said, "No one should ever criticize the man who breaks under prolonged torture, except to say that he shouldn't have let himself be captured alive in the first place. In our business, if an agent has information that's important and dangerous, it's taken for granted that he'll kill himself rather than be captured. He's given the stuff to do it with. It's the only sure way even a trained and loyal man, or woman, can keep from being made to talk."

Gail said, "And is this what you're going to do to me?"

I thought her voice sounded just a trifle shrill.

I shook my head. "I haven't the time or the facilities, and I don't think I need to."

"What does that mean?"

"Just what it says," I said. "I don't think I need to break you that way, Gail. An attractive woman is very vulnerable. The second form of torture is a kind of bargain. You tell the subject what you can do to him— or to her. You show that you're ready and willing to do it. And then you ask if he—or she—really is willing to have these unpleasant and fairly permanent things done to him—or to her—just for the sake of a little information that probably isn't very important, anyway."

She said, sharply, "You seem to think it's important enough!" Then she drew a long breath and said, "You wouldn't dare! If you really are a government man—"

I said, "For God's sake, Gail, make up your mind! If I'm really a government man, there's no problem, is there? You can tell me what you know with a clear conscience. In fact, it's your duty to do so." I waited. "Well?"

She glared at me. "Go to hell!"

I sighed, and leaned down, and picked up the ruined dress I had dropped on the rug. Ripped open down the side, with its broken straps dangling, it looked bedraggled and shapeless.

"Look at it, Gail," I said. "Five minutes ago, it was a pretty dress. Now it's just a rag. Right now you're a pretty woman. Five minutes from now…" I paused significantly.

"You bastard!" she whispered.

"I've seen it happen," I murmured. "One minute a lovely girl is standing there, resisting interrogation bravely, just like you, and the next minute there's just something half human crawling along the floor, something crippled and bloody and whimpering with its nose smashed flat in its face and its mouth full of broken teeth… Oh, I suppose they'll be able to fix you up eventually, Gail. They can do all kinds of things with dentistry and plastic surgery these days. But I doubt it would be much fun."

She crushed out her cigarette violently. "You bastard!" she breathed. "You filthy, sadistic bastard!"

I didn't say anything more. She wasn't sure, of course. I could still be bluffing. So far all I'd done was tear a dress; that didn't prove I had the ruthlessness to destroy a woman's face. But she wasn't a gambler; she couldn't take the chance. The stakes were too high. I didn't even have to put on a demonstration, although I had the arm of a chair picked out that I thought I might be able to crack with the edge of my hand. I saw her bare shoulders sag.

"You bastard," she said without looking at me, "does Wigwam mean anything to you, you filthy, sadistic bastard?"

"Wigwam?" I got out my pen and wrote it down. "Like an Indian tent?"

Gail didn't answer directly. "She said, 'Take it to the Wigwam in Carrizozo, New Mexico. The new date is December thirteenth.'"

"The Wigwam," I said, writing. "Carrizozo, New Mexico—I just drove through there today. December thirteenth."

"Stop interrupting me, damn you!" She didn't look at me. "Janie said that. Then she was quiet for a little. Then she said, 'December thirteenth. What's the date today? If it happens, I'll only have missed a few days, won't I, Gail? But you have to help them stop it…'"

"Have to help them stop it," I read from my notes. "Go on."

"That's all. Then she died." Gail's voice was flat. "Tell me… tell me, would you really have hit me, smashed me, or were you bluffing again?"

I hesitated. Of course I wouldn't have hit her. There would have been no point to it. If she'd been tough enough to refuse to talk, knowing what she might be facing, she'd have been too tough for me to handle here, particularly since I still didn't know if the matter was important enough to justify really drastic measures. I had the film safe, and the knowledge in her head would keep. If she'd stood firm, I'd just have checked with Washington. If they were interested, they could damn well send somebody with authority and official standing to pry it out of her legally.

But she hadn't been that tough, and I'd broken her with a threat, and a phony threat at that. It had been a shortcut, saving everybody time and trouble. She saw the answer in my face.

"Never mind!" she said quickly. "Don't answer that question! Just give me a drink and a dressing gown, please."

As I went to the closet and reached inside, somebody knocked twice on the door of the room.

8

I tossed aside the dressing gown I had taken down and got my gun from among my socks in the open suitcase at the foot of the bed. The knocking came again, a triple knock this time. It added up to a simple signal we sometimes use—two and three—to make sure the guy inside doesn't greet the guy outside with a bullet or a knife. That made it LeBaron, I figured, and I tucked my little snubnosed .38 under my belt and went over to open the door. Mac came in.

I closed the door behind him in a mechanical way. I was kind of startled, I guess. I mean, he doesn't get out in the field much. When you see him, normally, you see him behind his office desk—not that there's anything spectacular to see, just a lean, middle-aged gray-haired man with black eyebrows, wearing a gray suit as a rule, as he was today. Or you hear his voice over the phone or receive a message in code. You don't, on a job, expect to take time off to entertain him personally.

He didn't even glance at me. His face showed that he was looking for someone else, that he was very much concerned about that person's welfare. Then he spotted the slender woman standing there without a dress on—she wasn't exactly inconspicuous—and his lips compressed themselves tightly. He walked quickly to the bed, picked up the dressing gown I'd thrown aside and carried it over to her, holding it for her to put on. She slipped her arms through the sleeves and tied the belt at her waist.

"Mrs. Hendricks?" Mac said when she was decently covered.

She glanced at him quickly, surprised that he knew her name since she did not know his. "Yes. I'm Gail Hendricks."

"My name is Macdonald," he said. It wasn't. I'd learned his real name once, by accident, and it didn't even begin with Mac, but never mind that. He was still speaking with concern in his voice and manner. "When I learned that you'd been brought here against your will, I came at once, but it seems I've arrived too late to prevent…" He cleared his throat and glanced at the tattered blue dress I'd tossed over the back of a nearby chair—clear evidence that she hadn't disrobed voluntarily. Mac threw me a reproachful glance and said stiffly: "Sometimes my men exceed their orders, Mrs. Hendricks, I'm sorry to say…"

As he talked, I remained standing by the door, more or less at attention, like a private summoned from the ranks for disciplinary action. I didn't pay much attention to his words. I'd already heard enough to know which routine he was going to use. Instead, I amused myself by guessing where the nuke might be hidden.

He'd been listening, of course. His approach and timing were just a little too good to be true. He'd waited until I'd got everything out of her he wanted, and then he'd hurried in here to apologize and smooth things over, at my expense. Well, I could hardly blame him for not wanting to have a rich Texas female raising hell with her senators and congressmen.

Of course, I reflected, he could have saved himself the trouble by interrupting us at the very start of the proceedings. He could have broken it up and reprimanded me sternly for even considering such methods. He could have established his identity and asked for her patriotic cooperation—but he wouldn't have been Mac if he'd done that. This way he got a double check, first having me bully the information out of her, and then appearing himself, all consideration and apology, to gain her confidence and confirm that what she'd told me was the truth.

It was a beautiful example of the two-man interrogation technique, even though I hadn't known anybody was backing me up, but I couldn't help wondering exactly what he was doing here, two thousand miles from Washington, and how he'd come to have my hotel room bugged in the first place. After all, he hadn't been expecting me to bring this particular sister out of Juarez…

"You speak of your men," Gail was saying. "Just precisely who and what are you, Mr. Macdonald?"

Mac reached into his pocket. "Here, I think, is sufficient identification. You're entitled to see it, under the circumstances, but I must ask you to keep the information in strict confidence."

I watched her read the papers he'd given her. Presently she gave them back. "Of course I won't talk," she said. "But I don't understand… is this hoodlum really a government agent?"

Mac said quickly, "Mrs. Hendricks, you must understand, when men are trained for dangerous missions, when they are indoctrinated for violence, they sometimes find it hard to draw the line…"

"I see," she said. "Like savage dogs."

"If you want to put it like that. Actually, this is one of our best operatives. His name is Matthew Helm and he has done very good work…"

She wasn't following the summation for the defense. "And my sister," she said. "He said she was a member of the same outfit. Is that true?"

"Yes. At least, she was supposed to be."

There was a brief silence. Gail frowned. "Supposed to be. Just what does that mean?"

Mac said deliberately, "Mary Jane Springer, or Sarah as we knew her—that was her code name with us, as Mr. Helm's is Eric—was sent to Juarez after a certain individual who, we believe, is acting as an enemy agent and whose headquarters of sorts is in the Club Chihuahua. As you may know, this desolate southwestern country contains a good many secret government installations of great interest to the other side."

"I know," she said dryly. "I hear there's even a new

breed of radioactive jack rabbits out on the desert. They glow in the dark."

"Yes," Mac said. "Well, your sister was selected for the task of dealing with this man who was becoming troublesome to various people. Having been born in Texas, she knew the area well and spoke Spanish fluently. There were other considerations that helped make her a logical choice. However, after she'd been on the job for a while, another government agency, running checks on a certain security matter, sent the fingerprints and description of a suspect through channels. In due time, they reached my office in Washington. They tallied with the data in your sister's file."

"But—"

Mac went on, overriding the interruption. "I was not greatly disturbed, Mrs. Hendricks. This sort of thing happens. It only meant that, unknown to us, another agency had been watching the Club Chihuahua for other purposes, and Sarah's behavior had aroused their suspicions, which was only natural. I had a conference with the director of the agency in question, hoping to straighten things out so we wouldn't be working at cross purposes. He was very secretive—these security people are always hard to deal with—and he would give me no information whatever about his people or their activities in the area. He would not even give me access to the pertinent reports. He did, however, have excerpts made, which I compared with Sarah's reports. There were large discrepancies."

"Discrepancies?" Gail said. "What kind of discrepancies?"

"Sarah's accounts of her contacts and operations in the Club Chihuahua did not coincide at all with the accounts of the other operatives on the scene. In other words, somebody was sending in falsified reports."

"The other agency—"

"It's a possibility, of course, and they are checking the people involved. Meanwhile, I intercepted Mr. Helm, here, on his way east and diverted him to El Paso. He was to get your sister out of Juarez and bring her to this room." Mac rose and walked to a picture on the wall. He raised it to display the microphone underneath. "There are recording instruments next door. We like to have complete transcripts in cases like this. I flew in from Washington to conduct the interrogation myself. In our business, we cannot afford to take disloyalty lightly."

Gail licked her lips. "Why, you're assuming that Janie is… you're taking for granted she was guilty! Without proof!"

"Proof, Mrs. Hendricks?" Mac held out his hand towards me, palm up. I had the little film capsule ready, figuring he'd be wanting it sooner or later. I gave it to him. He held it out to show her. "Is any further proof needed? I might add, it wasn't entirely by accident that Mr. Helm was in the club at just that time. We had information that something of an incriminating nature might be passed, and that Sarah would act as the go-between. Our man likes to play safe, apparently. He prefers not to take delivery of dangerous materials directly."

"But—"

"I'm afraid there's no room for doubt. Mrs. Hendricks," Mac said. "It was a hard assignment. I would not have let Sarah take it on if she had not seemed quite certain she could handle it and eager to try. I believe revenge was a motive; I did not inquire too closely… Your sister was a rather difficult psychological case, you know. I have medical reports to the effect that her sexual attitudes were confused and immature. Normally, I pay little attention to such reports. I'm interested in the scores my people make on the target range; they can work out their sexual attitudes for themselves. But perhaps I should have given a little more weight to these reports, under the circumstances."

"I… I don't understand."

Mac said, "As I told you, your sister was ideally suited to the task in many respects—but most particularly because she was already acquainted with the man we were after, so there were none of the usual problems of identification and contact. But there was an emotional problem—it isn't easy for even a well-balanced woman to deal objectively and ruthlessly with a man with whom she has once been… shall we say, very close?"

Gail frowned quickly. "Close? You mean she'd known this man that well…?" Her voice stopped. Her eyes widened. She said, "My dear man, you can't be hinting that this mystery man of yours, this elusive enemy agent…?" She was silent again. Mac did not speak. She said flatly, "Sam? Sam Gunther?" Then she began to laugh.

9

She laughed and laughed. I guess it was nice to find something funny at last on this dreadful evening. There was also, no doubt, a little hysteria involved. After she'd gone on for a while I took a step forward with the thought of snapping her out of it, but Mac gave me the lay-off signal with a slight movement of his hand. He hadn't cracked a smile. I took my cue from him and waited with a perfectly straight face.

Her laughter died gradually. She sat down on the bed, wiping her eyes with the sleeve of my dressing gown, and looked up at Mac helplessly.

"My dear man," she gasped. "My dear man, if you knew how utterly ridiculous... Sam Gunther, of all people, the professional Texas charm boy!" She couldn't help giggling at the thought. "I'm sorry, Mr. Macdonald. Somebody's given you an awfully bum steer. Now, if you were after him for victimizing rich old ladies with his boyish grin, or getting some susceptible divorcee to pay his way from Reno to the Riviera... But Sam Gunther as the Master Spy in cowboy boots, why, that's just downright crazy!" She fought another giggle and lost.

"I'm sorry that I can't share your amusement, Mrs. Hendricks," Mac said. His voice was cold. "I may be prejudiced, but I always find it difficult to see anything humorous about a man who has killed one of my operatives."

She stared at him, shocked. I said quickly, "LeBaron?"

Mac nodded. "Shot in the chest at close range. He was taken to the hospital in Juarez. He died without gaining consciousness. For a mere gigolo, Mr. Gunther seems to be handy with firearms."

I started to speak but stopped. I'd been going to ask if LeBaron had been warned the opposition was dangerous, but it would have been a silly question. We're not supposed to have to be warned, and a man with a gun is always dangerous.

Gail Hendricks licked her lips. "It... was an accident, I'm sure. Sam was just trying to help me. He didn't know—"

Mac said, "LeBaron was a trained man, Mrs. Hendricks. He had received thorough instructions in how to deal with an armed opponent. I prefer not to believe that he met his death by clumsy accident."

Those were just words, of course. The only really effective way to deal with an armed opponent who keeps his head, if you haven't got a gun yourself, is to place a solid obstacle between you and him and run like hell. But if Mac wanted to make a point, I wasn't going to spoil it with awkward technical details. It did seem to me we were telling this woman a lot of stuff she had no business knowing, but I couldn't complain about that, either, since I'd started it. I presumed Mac had some plan for keeping her mouth shut.

I heard my own voice. "Where's Gunther now?"

Mac glanced at me. "He has disappeared. The border is being watched."

I made a rude sound. "It's a thousand-mile border. Who's going to watch it all?"

Gail was shaking her head. "I still can't believe… Sam isn't my favorite person by any means, but—"

"There seems to be no doubt about it," Mac said. "Washington has been trying for years to identify an enemy operative who goes by the code name of Cowboy… What amuses you now, Mrs. Hendricks?"

"If it's Sam, he certainly dresses the part."

"That could be his way of thumbing his nose at all the agencies that have been trying to discover his identity, flaunting his big hat and cowboy boots as he goes about his work. Even a clever agent will often allow himself a small touch of arrogance. Of course, it is always a weakness, sometimes a fatal one."

"Well, I never rated Sam as very clever," Gail said. "And aren't you forgetting something, Mr. Macdonald? Maybe he's been to the Club Chihuahua before for other reasons—I don't know about that—but he was there tonight because I brought him. He wasn't eager to go."

"Very probably he wasn't eager to go with you, Mrs.
Hendricks," Mac said. "Your insistence upon visiting
the club in his company at just this time must have
been awkward from his point of view; naturally, he was
reluctant."

"But—"

"I wouldn't be too eager to take responsibility for Mr.
Gunther's presence, Mrs. Hendricks," Mac said smoothly.
"As the person who accompanied him to the scene, you're
already in a rather unfortunate position. I thought, of
course, that you would claim to be an innocent dupe.
They always do."

She frowned. "They? Who?"

"The legal term is accomplice, I believe."

There was a moment of silence. Her eyes widened.
"My dear man, what are you driving at?" she demanded.

"My dear lady," he said, using the form of address
deliberately, "consider the facts. Your sister, unfortunately
dead so she cannot be questioned, was undoubtedly
working as a double agent. That is, still maintaining a
pretense of working for us, but actually betraying us to
the other side. Whether she succumbed to Mr. Gunther's
physical attractions a second time, or whether he used
other means of persuasion, doesn't matter for the moment.
She was helping him, and she was doing it voluntarily—"

"How do you know that?"

Mac said patiently, "She was still sending in reports.
There are certain signs, certain signals, for an agent to
use when his reports are prepared under duress, or when

he knows they will be read by the enemy and is therefore making them deliberately misleading. No such signals showed up in your sister's communications… I think we may take it as established that for one reason or another she had gone over to the enemy, or at least to Mr. Gunther."

"Then why was she killed?"

Mac moved his shoulders. "It is a common fate of double agents. They walk a narrow and uncertain path, knowing too much about both sides. They are expendable." He paused. "Now let's examine your part in tonight's proceedings, Mrs. Hendricks. At a critical moment, you arrived in the club with Mr. Gunther. You admit you brought him; he did not bring you?"

She hesitated. "Well, as a matter of fact, he did suggest that the ten-thirty show—"

"I see," Mac said dryly. "So now Mr. Gunther has some say in the matter. It is no longer entirely your idea."

She said angrily, "I don't like your attitude at all! There's no need to start acting like a prosecuting attorney!"

Mac shrugged. "I'm afraid you're going to have to get used to prosecuting attorneys, Mrs. Hendricks. You're apt to meet quite a few of them in the near future."

She was on her feet, aghast. "What do you mean? I haven't done anything! You can't think—"

"What I think," Mac said gently, "or what Mr. Helm thinks, is quite beside the point. The facts speak for themselves. You arrived at the Club Chihuahua at precisely the strategic time. When things went wrong, you were quick to take the secret material from your

sister and receive her instructions. When an agent of
the U.S. Government asked you, a loyal citizen, to turn
this material and information over to him, you refused
to cooperate, forcing him to resort to violence and
intimidation. His actions weren't quite legal, perhaps, but
I doubt that he'll be condemned for excessive zeal, under
the circumstances."

"But how could I believe him?" she demanded. "He
had no identification, no—"

"Mrs. Hendricks, the taped record in the next room will
show that Mr. Helm, before resorting to other means, did
everything in his power to convince you of his genuineness,
even to taking oath on the Holy Bible. I'm sorry, but I'm
afraid you'll have to consider yourself under arrest."

She gasped. I refrained from looking in his direction. I
suppose we can arrest people if we have to—any citizen
can, under certain conditions—but we don't make a habit
of it. He was throwing a scare into her for some reason.
Standard procedure required that, now that he was taking
the heavy part, I should suffer an abrupt change of heart
in the subject's favor.

I said, "Sir, I don't really think—"

He glanced at me impatiently. "What is it, Eric?"

"Isn't it possible that Mrs. Hendricks has been just…
well, a little naïve and foolish?"

He said, "That may be, but let's be practical. One of
our agents has gone over to the enemy—this woman's
sister. Even though the girl is now dead, it puts us in a
very bad light. Do you understand? We are also going

to have to report the loss of a second agent, and the unpalatable fact that important government secrets have been compromised. The wolves in Washington will want blood. Well, let them chew on Mrs. Hendricks, while we continue our task of locating and dealing with the real villain. She was given every chance to cooperate and she refused. Innocent or guilty, she has earned no consideration from us."

"But, sir, in all fairness—"

Gail Hendricks made an impatient gesture. "Oh, stop that silly dialogue. You don't fool me one little bit, either of you. You're both... both equally despicable!" She faced Mac defiantly. "If that microphone you showed me is working, how is the little speech you just made going to sound on your precious tapes?"

Mac spread his hands. "My dear lady, it will never be heard. If the technician was fool enough to record it... well, magnetic tapes are easy to erase and edit."

"I see." Her hands were clenched into fists. Her face was white. "It's just a frame-up, is that it?"

"My dear lady—"

She made a strangled sound. "If you call me that again, I... I'll scream!" There was a little silence. She glanced at me quickly. "What are you grinning at, you elongated ape?"

I didn't answer. As a matter of fact, I wasn't grinning. Mac said, "We are merely doing our duty, Mr. Hendricks, reporting matters bearing on national security that have come to our attention. I will send in no information that is not absolutely accurate, believe me. I may delete a few items I consider irrelevant, but that hardly constitutes a frame-up."

She touched her lips with her tongue. "You're being stupid and ridiculous, you know that, don't you? Nobody'll believe for a minute—"

"No?" Mac opened his hand and showed her the little film capsule again. "Less spectacular evidence than this sent Alger Hiss to the penitentiary and the Rosenbergs to the electric chair, Mrs. Hendricks. Would you like to see what is on this film you carried hidden on your person and refused to surrender?"

She hesitated and licked her lips again. "Yes."

Mac studied her face for a moment. Then he pried open the small cartridge, and spoke without turning his head.

"Eric, you have a magnifier, haven't you?"

I got it for him. He examined the film strip briefly, and passed it to Gail, with the glass. She frowned and squinted and moved the lens back and forth helplessly.

"Just hold it next to your eye," I said, "and bring the films up into focus. It's customary to look towards the light."

She gave me an angry look, but followed instructions. I saw her get a sharp image at last. A startled expression came to her face.

"But this is—"

Mac said, "You undoubtedly have read about the project in the newspapers. It is known, picturesquely, as Operation Mole: the underground atomic explosion to be set off shortly in the Manzanita Mountains, not too far north in New Mexico. We've had hints that there might be trouble about it."

"But—"

Mac went on: "What you have in your hands is a set of unauthorized copies of the basic instructions covering Operation Mole, as revised following a recent postponement. There is, you will note, a detailed diagram of the underground chamber in which the explosion will take place, as well as a map of the area showing the relative locations of the chamber and the above-ground monitoring station in the foothills a safe distance away where a group of selected observers will be with Dr. Rennenkamp, the director of the project and his staff. There are also a copy of the orders, two pages, covering the general security measures to be taken and a summary of the time schedule for the operation. Note the new date, December thirteenth, the date mentioned by your sister, according to your recorded testimony. This date, let me point out, has not yet been made public."

She started to speak, then was silent. Mac took the film and began to roll it up carefully.

"Well, Mrs. Hendricks, what do you think? If you were on a jury, shown this evidence, and told where it was found, and if you heard how extremely reluctant the bearer was to part with it, what would your verdict be?"

She hesitated. "All right," she whispered. "All right, damn you! It's blackmail, isn't it? You want something, don't you? What do you want me to do?"

10

In the morning, it was snowing. To hear the Texans in the hotel lobby, this was a big thing in El Paso history. It snows every so often in El Paso, but they always act as if each time was the first in the memory of man. The clerk at the desk considered me foolish even to think of venturing out into the dangerous stuff. The very idea of driving north into the white wilderness of New Mexico, he said, was suicidal. The little town of Carrizozo, to hear him tell it, was as inaccessible, for the moment, as Point Barrow, Alaska.

When I came outside, after that build-up, expecting snowdrifts to the second story, I found the streets merely wet and black with big soft white flakes drifting out of the gray sky and a little slush building up where the traffic left it alone. I asked the doorman to retrieve my truck from the parking garage across the street and went back inside just in time to see Gail Hendricks emerging from the elevator, followed by a bellboy loaded with my luggage and hers which had been brought over from a motel, earlier.

She was certainly decorative, I reflected, watching her approach. The arrangement of her light-brown hair was still kind of elaborately loose and fluffy, but this morning she was quite simply dressed in a pleated skirt and a cashmere sweater that was neither sexy tight nor sloppy loose. It was blue and matched the subdued plaid of the skirt. A single strand of pearls dressed things up a bit. She was carrying a kind of twill greatcoat with a luxurious fur lining. I guess the height of snobbishness is wearing your mink so it doesn't show.

I said, "Good morning," in a neutral way as she came up. I had no idea what her attitude was going to be, except that it would probably be very hostile.

She surprised me by speaking quite reasonably. "You're exaggerating, aren't you, Mr. Helm? It doesn't look like a very good morning to me." She frowned at the snowflakes drifting past the door to melt on the sidewalk. "Do you think it's safe to start out? What if it keeps up all day?"

"That's my brave *tejano* partner, Gail the fearless and intrepid," I said. "I keep forgetting that all Texas comes to a shivering standstill when it snows."

She made a face at me. "You can't blame me for not being anxious to make this trip. It wasn't my idea, remember?"

"I remember," I said. "But you seem more resigned to the idea than you were last night."

She laughed and shrugged. "What's the saying? You can't buck city hall, isn't that right?"

She held out the big coat. I helped her on with it. We walked out, followed by the bellboy. I had him put the luggage into the bed of the pickup, which was protected by an aluminum canopy—not one of those fancy, trailer-like jobs, with stove, sink, and refrigerator, just a weatherproof shelter back there with windows and a door. There was space enough to sleep on an old cot mattress, even with all my camping gear aboard and generous headroom for sitting but not for standing. At the moment, it was the nearest thing to a home I owned.

I paid the storage charges, distributed tips all around, helped Gail inside, and we were off—blast-off time, approximately eight-forty-five. After a while, my companion, relaxing beside me, lit a cigarette and blew smoke at the windshield. Her resigned attitude bothered me a little. I hadn't thought she was a woman to take coercion in such a docile fashion, and neither had Mac.

We have three things to work with, he'd said late last night when we were planning the operation, *a place in Carrizozo, a film capsule and a lady who hates us but knows Gunther, perhaps better than we think. Put them all together and we may have a productive combination. It's the best we can do with the limited time at our disposal.*

Men were working in Mexico, of course, following the trail. There was an agent on his way to Midland, Gunther's home town, and the motel where Gunther had stayed with Gail was being watched, but that was none of my concern.

My job was to deal with him if he came to Carrizozo, one possibility out of many, but we thought a good one.

"Matt," Gail said abruptly. "I'd better start calling you Matt, hadn't I?"

"Permission granted."

"I just don't get it, Matt," she went on. "Do we just walk up to this Wigwam place and march in the front door, or what? And those films, how are we supposed to use them? I suppose they're still valuable to somebody."

They were, of course, so valuable that they were on their way to Washington right now. Even Mac didn't swing enough weight to authorize one of his men to walk around with national secrets in his shoes, not without consulting a lot of important people first, so we had decided that, for bait, if I got a chance to use it, the capsule itself would have to do. But there was no need for her to know that.

"We don't know exactly how valuable they are," I said. "We can only hope the other side still wants them badly. It's a pretty scrambled mess of an operation, Gail. Normally, two agents on a job like this would have rehearsed their cover stories for weeks in advance. As it is, we're going to have to size up the situation when we get there, and improvise like hell."

"And it's really Sam Gunther you're after? It's… absolutely crazy! Why, I've known him for years!"

"People had known Klaus Fuchs for years. They thought him a nice, harmless sort of guy, I've heard."

"If you catch him…" She hesitated. "When you catch him, what happens then?"

She had a knack of bringing up awkward subjects. I said, "Well, that kind of depends on Sam." Well, it did, to a certain extent.

She said, "I'd hate to be the one responsible for… for getting him killed, or anything."

I glanced at her. "The man is a murderer and a traitor, Gail. Both crimes carry the death penalty." It didn't seem necessary or diplomatic to point out that somewhere in the hierarchy above Mac sentence had already been passed on Sam Gunther, who was known as the Cowboy. People outside the business don't like to think things are done that way, and it's best to leave them their illusions whenever possible, but I told Gail as much of the truth as I thought she could stand. "Whatever happens, if we're successful in our mission, Sam isn't likely to survive it very long. You might as well face that now."

We drove for a while in silence. She was looking straight ahead through the wet windshield. At last she said, "It's not… a very nice thing to face. It won't be a very nice thing to live with."

I said, "Well, you can look at it one of two ways. Either you're a brave lady patriot helping to dispose of your country's enemy at the risk of your life, or you're a cheap female Judas sending a man you know to his death to save your own skin. Take your choice."

Her head came around sharply. "Damn you! You didn't have to say that!"

"Don't be a fool," I said. "Of course I had to say it. It's what he'll say if he gets a chance, isn't it?"

She hesitated then drew a long breath. "Yes, but you've got such a lousy, brutal way of putting things, darling." She glanced aside and spoke in an even voice. "I suppose you know you're on the wrong road. This highway leads to Las Cruces. We're supposed to be heading for Alamogordo, on the way to Carrizozo, aren't we?"

I said, "Yes, but I thought I'd take that fellow behind us for a little scenic ride, first. His persistence certainly deserves some kind of a reward."

It took her a moment to catch the meaning of what I'd said; then she started to swing around in her seat.

"No, don't look back," I said. "Use the mirror."

She turned to an outside mirror. The truck sported two, one on each side, since visibility through the canopy was limited. She had to lean forward to get the proper angle. "The gray Olds sedan," I said, "two cars back."

She licked her lips. "You mean... somebody is following us?"

"Tailing is the technical word," I said. "Yes, somebody's tailing us. He picked us up right around the corner from the hotel. How's your geography, Gail?"

"I don't know... This road goes on up the Rio Grande Valley, doesn't it?"

"That's right," I said. "And the road we want goes up the Tularosa Valley on the other side of those mountains coming up on the right. For the moment, of course, we don't know anybody's behind us. We're just plugging northward innocently..."

"But shouldn't we find a phone and call Mr. Macdonald

before we're too far out in the country?"

I thought of what Mac would say if one of his people called up in a sweat merely because somebody, mysterious and menacing, was trailing along behind.

"He's on his way back to Washington, if his plane ever got off," I said. "We're kind of supposed to take care of ourselves. Besides, I'd like to find out what instructions the gent back there is carrying."

I looked around. We were well out of El Paso now, traveling across a flat country flecked with snow that looked wet and gray in the bad light. The mountains to our right rose up into the low clouds. The higher visible slopes were solidly white; it was coming down more heavily up there.

I said, "In Las Cruces, some fifty miles ahead, if he hasn't made a move by then, I'll stop to have the tank filled and the tire chains put on. Let's hope our friend is a good Texan. If he is, he'll have a childlike faith in his snow tires and an abiding distaste for chains. When I lived in Santa Fe, farther north in New Mexico, we used to lose more Texans off the road to the nearby ski run. Even the cops couldn't make them put chains on." I glanced at the mirror. The gray Oldsmobile had dropped back a little now that we were on the open highway, but it was still coming right along. I said, "Leaving Las Cruces, I'll suddenly discover that we've got company. I'll put on speed, pathetically trying to outrun that guy's three hundred horsepower with this old relic. Failing, I'll swing abruptly to the east and head over the pass towards White

Sands and Alamogordo and the road we really want. Have you done any sports car driving, Gail? Do you know what it means to hit the cellar?"

"Well, I've ridden in them, of course, and driven a few, but they're mostly so dreadfully uncomfortable and impractical—"

"Sure," I said. It was no time for an argument on that subject. I pointed to the worn rubber mat under our feet. "Well, there's your storm cellar. I want you to have your coat buttoned and your hood up; that'll give you some protection. If we start to go and I give the word, you dive for the floor and cover your face with your arms. Got it?"

She had turned pale. "If we start to... What do you mean?"

I said patiently, "Look, glamor girl, we'll cross a pass, San Agustin Pass, elevation damn close to six thousand feet." I pointed. "It's up there somewhere, but you can't see it for the clouds. Beyond, there's a nice stretch of mountain road heading into the other valley, with quite a steep drop-off on the outside, the side we'll be on going down. It'll probably be snowing pretty heavily up there. There'll be fog by the looks of it. The visibility will be real lousy, so a gent with criminal intentions won't have to worry much about witnesses. We're carrying something somebody's supposed to want, remember? Looking at it one way, this is a very encouraging sign, that they're taking such an interest in us already."

"But—"

"That lad behind us has a big, heavy, powerful car,"

I said. "If he's got orders to do something about this old pickup of mine, something that looks accidental, say, so he'll have a chance to search the bodies—up there's where he'll probably make his play."

"You mean—" Her voice was strained. "You mean he'll try to run us off the road up there?"

I glanced at her and saw something that surprised me—she had freckles. It was completely out of character, but there they were, a faint dusting of color across the bridge of her nose.

I said, "Your freckles show when you're scared, Gail. It's kind of cute…"

As murder attempts go, it was kind of pitiful. The Olds was in sight behind us during the long grind up the pass until the murk got too thick to see anything. I turned on my lights to make things easy for him. We topped out at just under six thousand feet and started down through the clouds on the other side. He waited until the road emerged on the open flank of the mountain. Then he came roaring out of the snow and mist behind us and swung over to give us the nudge that would send us off the edge—blasting away with his horn to terrify us, I suppose, or to make us stop and get out of the car with our hands up.

I hit the brakes and my tire chains took hold at once. With nothing but rubber to stop him, he was past before he could connect, skidding badly. I saw his face looking at us. The glass was blurred with condensed moisture, but I recognized the sallow face and thin black mustache of the M.C. of the Club Chihuahua.

I threw a fast downshift into second gear and fed power to the rear wheels. The chains found traction in the new direction, and the old truck lurched forward, digging out hard downhill. For a moment, the touch, as we call it in the business, looked possible. He was right in position ahead, now in a bad slide to the left, having over-corrected his first wild skid. The whole flank of the big car was open and vulnerable. If I could only gain enough relative speed before the impact, it ought to slew him around broadside in front of me and also swing the truck around to the right just about the proper amount. I was ready then to slam the lever into that stump-pulling reserve low-gear that comes with a heavy-duty truck transmission and bulldoze him right off the edge.

"Down," I said, without turning my head. "Hit the basement. Cover your face."

I mean, there was bound to be a bump, and there was even a possibility that we'd go over with him if I miscalculated. Then the little man got off his brake. Only a flat-lander would have braked so hard in the first place, coming down a slick mountain road without chains. The glowing taillights went out, and the big sedan, wheels no longer locked, straightened out and surged ahead, presenting me with nothing but a massive chrome bumper to shoot at.

Hitting him there was useless, even if I could catch up with him—I'd just be shoving him down the road ahead of me. So I eased up on the gas and watched him pull away into the mist. Gail, I realized, had made no move towards the floor.

I said, "Sixty-one Olds hard-top four-door, gray, one aboard. Texas license DD 2109. Write it down, please. There's a pad and pencil in the glove compartment." After quite a long time, she reached out and opened the compartment clumsily. I said, "We may see more of him later. I suppose he was after the films—unless he's just one of those unreasonable guys who get sore when you kick them in a certain place. You recognized him from the club, I suppose—the little runt of an M.C. with a Spanish accent who was telling the girls to take it off." Her voice was shaky. "No. No, I didn't see him. I... I wasn't looking." She hesitated, then said with a show of defiance, "As a matter of fact, I had my eyes closed."

"Your ears, too?" I said. "I told you to get down."

"I... I couldn't move," she said. "I just couldn't, Matt!"

"Sure," I said. "Well, we'll stop for lunch in Alamogordo. You can change into dry panties there."

Her face came around sharply. She gave me a glance of pure hatred, started to speak but checked herself with an effort. After a moment, she turned away, looking straight ahead.

"I'm sorry," she whispered, stiff-lipped. "I know I'm not very... Don't be too hard on me, darling. I'm not used to this sort of thing."

Her meekness was as phony as a drunk's New Year's resolution. She would have loved to cut my throat with a dull knife, but she was saving me for a more elaborate and excruciating fate. At least I hoped that was what was behind the phony humility.

A woman who hates you, Mac had said. Then he continued thoughtfully, *Of course you can't trust her, but untrustworthy people can sometimes be very useful. There was a case during the war, if you recall, where the whole operation hinged upon one agent's known weakness...*

We were being very clever, not to say diabolical. We were counting on this woman to hate, despise, and, given the opportunity, betray me—it was a desperate plan, but there was no time to be careful. I couldn't take a chance on lousing up the job by letting her develop any respect or affection for me. Well, there wasn't much chance of that.

11

In Alamogordo, the cafe that served us lunch made up a stack of sandwiches for us and filled a Thermos with coffee. What with the gin and tequila I'd bought in Juarez, I figured we were well prepared to cope with any blizzard straying this far south. Up north, of course, where they blow for days and involve temperatures far below zero, you have to take them more seriously.

The weather was getting mean when we came outside. Snow, driven by a rising wind, was falling heavily. When we got out of town, we discovered that every damn fool in the country with a slick set of tires and no brains had picked this stretch of highway to demonstrate his stupidity. It took us almost an hour to cover the twelve miles from Alamogordo to Tularosa, mainly because of the stalled traffic. That left us with forty-five miles to go to Carrizozo. By five o'clock we still hadn't made it, and I was getting pretty tired of fighting it. The snow was nothing, but the morons blocking the road were enough to drive you crazy.

I found a ranch road leading off to the right. The unbroken snow indicated that nobody'd been over it since the storm started. I turned off the highway and headed in. Progress was slow, and coming out again would be a problem if the weather held, but on the other hand, nobody was going to follow us through that stuff in an ordinary passenger car, with or without chains. I had no intention of standing guard all night. I'd worry about getting out when the time came.

The road turned down into a gully containing clumps of desert evergreens. I had the lights on, but the visibility was terrible, and I had trouble deciding where I was supposed to go from there. It was all snow. I said to hell with it, stopped, rocked the pickup back and forth a bit when it wouldn't come loose at once, and backed it in among the nearest trees. I cut the lights and windshield wipers, leaving the engine and heater running.

"I hope you know what you're doing," Gail said, beside me. Her voice sounded rusty from disuse.

I said, "A guy tried to run us off a cliff, remember? He may be a hundred miles away by now, but I'd rather not bank on it. Those tracks will be drifted over in half an hour, enough so in the dark nobody'll know we're here."

"That's nice," she said. "I suppose somebody'll find our bodies, come spring."

I said, "You must lead a hell of a life, glamor girl, terrorized by every little snowflake. Look, the highway is only about a mile due west. If we can't get the truck out in the morning, we'll just dress up warmly and walk out for help. Okay? Now take your shoes off and make yourself comfortable… Oh, and you can take that wary look off your face, too."

"I wasn't—"

"The arrangements," I said, "will be simple and virtuous. You'll sleep up front here in the cab. The seat's a little short, but you'll come a lot closer to fitting in than I would. I'll bed down in back. Now, with that great load off your mind, suppose you tell me whether you prefer gin or tequila with your ham sandwich…"

I brought the refreshments out of the rear, switched on the interior light, and we had a kind of picnic there in the cab while the storm-lashed twilight outside gradually turned black with premature night. Over the rumble of the motor and the whir of the heater keeping us warm, we could hear the wind screaming through the nearby trees.

It was cozy enough in the truck, but it was kind of like being alone in space, hurtling along a predetermined orbit in a sealed capsule. I saw the attractive woman at the other end of the seat wince as the truck rocked on its springs, feeling the blast. I reached out and poured a couple of fingers of tequila into her plastic cup.

"Didn't you ever sit out a blue norther before?" I asked. "I thought you told me you were born on a ranch."

She shrugged. "I never was any more of an outdoors girl than I had to be." Her eyes narrowed. "Come to think of it, darling, I never told you anything of the sort. Have you been checking up on me?"

"Did you think we wouldn't? The dope came through

just before breakfast. Just a brief summary."

She laughed shortly. "It must have made interesting reading."

As a matter of fact, it hadn't. It had been the usual story of a girl with too much beauty, too much money and too many husbands.

"I must say," she said, "that the idea of people snooping around and asking questions—"

She stopped, as a violent gust swept through our sheltering hollow. A branch beat against the side of the metal canopy. Snow peppered the windshield like thrown gravel. From inside, the glass looked crystallized and opaque. Gail's knuckles were white, gripping the cup.

"Relax," I said. "The end of the world should still be a few days off, if my guess is correct."

She said, "Damn you, we can't all be great pioneer heroes… What did you mean by that?"

"I've been thinking," I said, "about Sarah—your sister Janie, and what made her do it, go over, as we call it. Mac isn't often so wrong about the people he picks. Screwy as we are, we don't usually let him down for reasons of simple biological attraction. She wasn't a school kid, after all. She'd had training and a couple of years' experience in a tough racket."

"Yes," Gail said. "One day I'm going to find out exactly how tough this racket of yours is, darling." It could have been a veiled threat, although her face showed no hint of it.

I said, "I figure he must have pulled the old doomsday pitch on her. It's the one they usually drag out when it's a question of nuclear weapons and they need a few misguided idealists to throw sand in the works. It explains what she said to you when she was dying."

"You mean, about her only missing a few days?"

I nodded. "That's the way I read it. The world is going to end December thirteenth, she'd been told, presumably due to this underground test in the Manzanitas, if she didn't do something about it quick or get you to do it for her... Well, they've pulled that line before and the world's still here, so I'm not going to brood about it. I'll get you a sleeping bag. Which suitcase do you want?" She hesitated, started to ask a question then changed her mind. "The small one has my nightie—"

"Nightie?" I said. "What do you think this is, a June honeymoon at Niagara Falls? You'll freeze to death in a nylon nightie. You'd better sleep in those clothes or pull on some warm slacks if you've got them; you may even have to keep your coat on. It'll get cold in here when we shut down the motor. If you haven't got wool socks, I'll lend you a pair."

She said, rather stiffly, "I'll wear my own things, thank you."

"Suit yourself," I said. "Sleep well."

12

It took her more than an hour to make up her mind and then having made it up, to do something about it. Lying in back, I saw the cab light come on, illuminating the window above my head. A lot of activity followed— when a greenhorn gets involved with a sleeping bag, you'd think a boa constrictor had got into the act.

At last the light went out and the cab door opened— and closed noisily, slammed shut by the wind. Seconds later, she was knocking at the rear door of the canopy. I let her wait a little. It wouldn't do to let her think I'd been expecting her. Finally, I made a grudging sound and crawled back to raise the door which was hinged at the top and swung up like a station-wagon transom.

"Here," she said, pushing an armload of bedding at me. I disposed of the stuff behind me and reached down to help her inside.

"Watch your head," I said. "This isn't the lobby of the Hotel Paso del Norte. What's the matter?"

"I'm freezing up there," she gasped, scrambling in beside me. "And scared."

"I offered you warm socks. And I told you to wear your coat."

"There wasn't room for it inside that damn zipper bag. And when I spread it over me, it kept falling off. Anyway, you can't talk to a damn coat."

I closed and latched the door, shutting out the snow and wind. I switched on the electric lantern I kept back there, got her sleeping bag open like a blanket and wrapped it around her shoulders. She drew it tight about her, shivering realistically. I found the tequila bottle and the plastic cups.

"We're going to die!" she moaned tragically, taking the cup I offered her. "We're never going to get out of this dreadful place alive!"

I laughed. "Cut it out. Now if we'd counted on staying in a motel, we'd be in real trouble. There aren't many along this highway, and they'll all be full of stranded travelers, tonight."

"My feet!" she said. "They're frozen absolutely solid."

"Sure," I said. "Gangrene will set in any minute." I made an examination. She'd come around the truck in her stocking feet, rather than ruin her shoes in the snow. "You'd better take off those wet nylons," I said.

She hesitated then unwrapped herself enough to get her skirt up and one garter disengaged; then she began to shake uncontrollably and hugged the robe about her again. Well, she probably was kind of cold. I wouldn't have wanted to run around out there practically barefoot. "You d-do it," she gasped.

I glanced at her. She had the grace to blush. It was pretty damn corny. I mean, I hadn't been sure until then—not absolutely sure—but the please-help-me-off-with-my-stockings gambit was a dead give-away. No adult woman who didn't plan on getting laid was going to start *that* routine—alone with a man in a cramped refuge on a stormy night.

"Sure," I said. "Anything to oblige, ma'am."

I got on my knees and arranged the lantern for better visibility. I prepared the patient for the operation. After a little, she laughed softly, watching me work.

"Does it bother you, undressing a woman, Matt?" She didn't seem to be shivering so much any more. "No, that's right, you're the iron man, aren't you? The unfeeling brute who strips them and searches them without a thought for anything but duty and country." There was malice in her voice.

I shook out a transparent nylon stocking and draped it over a pile of stuff at the side. "Would it have made you feel better if I'd raped you?" I asked.

She laughed again. "In a way, of course it would. It would have meant you were looking at me as a woman instead of as a suspicious character." She watched me work the other stocking down and slip it off her foot. When she spoke, her voice was quite different, very soft, very gentle. "You don't have to stop with the stockings, darling. You know that."

"Yes," I said. "I know it."

There was a little silence inside the canopy, while outside the storm whistled and howled. For some reason I was stalling. I drew a long breath and looked at my watch.

"What's the matter?" she asked, rather sharply. "What are you doing?"

"Just checking the time," I said. "I've got a bet riding on this." I didn't but it seemed like a good line. I don't like sex under false pretenses. Sometimes you have to do it that way, in the business, but tonight I couldn't see that it was necessary. "Five bucks," I said.

There was another little silence. When she spoke, her voice was absolutely flat. "Five bucks?" she said, "On what?"

"On whether or not we're making love by nine o'clock," I said, which was another lie. We'd discussed the probability, Mac and I, but no time had been mentioned. "It's all right," I said. "My money's safe. We've still got forty minutes to go."

There was another stretch of silence, but it didn't last long. I was ready for her when she came at me, striking at my face with her nails. I got her wrists, as I had once before. She was strong enough, for a woman, but she had no conception of the use of leverage.

"Easy now," I said. "Take it easy, glamor girl. You'll only hurt yourself."

"You beast!" she gasped. "You… you creature! You contemptible—"

"Sure," I said. "There wasn't any bet, Gail. I was just

kidding." She didn't speak, breathing heavily, and I said, "You were pretty corny, you know, with that stocking routine. I had to shake you up a bit."

"You louse! You stinking, miserable—" She stopped abruptly and spoke in that perfectly flat voice: "I don't understand."

"Truce?" I said, still holding her.

After a moment, she nodded. I released her wrists, and she sat there rubbing them, not looking at me, while the truck rocked on its spring and hard little pellets of wind-driven snow rattled against the aluminum canopy. I thought the weather would probably break by morning. That hard buckshot snow generally comes with the end of the storm.

"I don't understand," Gail said again.

"You shouldn't try to seduce a man my age with such obvious tricks, glamor girl," I said. "It hurts his pride. Also, there was a matter of principle. There wasn't any bet, but, last night my chief and I did discuss your possible reactions. The consensus was that you'd probably try this. I thought you ought to know that we'd talked about it."

She licked her lips. "You discussed... You actually talked about whether or not I'd... What in the world made you think...?"

"Cut it out," I said. "Can't you see I'm trying to keep this on a reasonably honest basis? Don't go hypocritical on me, Gail."

She hesitated, then said in a different voice: "Did I give myself away that badly?"

"You didn't have to. It was obvious that you hated us, me in particular. God knows, you had plenty of reason. It seemed inevitable that somewhere on this trip you'd try to get even, somehow. And how is a woman going to get even with a man who's too big for her to beat up and has all the resources of the U.S. Government behind him?"

She started to speak, then stopped. Presently she said, "You're a funny person. All right, and where are we now?"

"In the back of a truck in a blizzard," I said, "slowly turning to solid ice while you make up your mind where and how you're going to spend the night."

Her head came up. She stared at me. "You're not really conceited enough, are you, to think I'd still consider…?" I didn't say anything, and presently she laughed. It was a real laugh, soft and warm and kind of nice. "Oh, hell," she said, "I'm certainly not going to wade back through three feet of snow to that cast-iron front seat, and if I stay here you'll probably ravish me before morning, anyway."

I said, "Damn, I hate women who think they're irresistible. Do you want me to sleep in the cab, just to prove something?"

She said, "No, darling, I think you've proved quite enough for one night. Well, *almost* quite enough…"

13

The first thing I noticed, waking, was the silence. There wasn't a sound anywhere, inside or outside the truck, except for the quiet breathing of the woman in my arms.

Gail stirred sleepily and burrowed closer. The temperature must have dropped twenty degrees during the night—as it often does out there right after a storm. I stuck my head out of the covers and saw there was light under the canopy. The windows were white with frost. I summoned my courage and squirmed out from under the sleeping bag and blankets piled on top of us, tucking them back around Gail. I put on coat, hat, and boots, and opened my suitcase to find a pair of gloves.

I found them all right and stopped in the middle of pulling them on, looking at a small, unfamiliar, paper-wrapped package tucked in among my belongings. The printing on the wrapper said: RODRIGUEZ CURIOS, JUAREZ, MEXICO. I hesitated, pulled off the gloves again, opened the package and looked at the rolled-up belt inside—

obviously a farewell gift from Mac, something he thought I might be needing on this job.

It looked innocent enough, just a handcarved leather belt with a heavy, ornate buckle. It was, I knew, almost as innocent as it looked. There were no secret compartments, no razor blades concealed between strips of leather, no steel spring knives or saws. The only gimmick was the buckle, carefully designed to serve a number of purposes, some quite lethal. It was a grim reminder that I hadn't come here to play amorous games in the snow.

"Good morning, darling," Gail's voice said behind me. "Is it as cold as I think it is?"

"Colder," I said. "You stay wrapped up until I get the cab warm. How's the glamor girl this morning?"

"She never felt less glamorous," Gail laughed. "I'd make a terrible Eskimo; I like to take my clothes off when I go to bed… What have you got there?"

"Just something I picked up in Juarez."

The falsehood was a little harder to manage convincingly, I noticed, than it would have been the previous day. I dropped the open package in front of her.

"Oh, a belt," she said, and let it lie rather than expose herself to the cold by reaching out to investigate. "I don't like those damn big fancy cowboy belts. I think a man looks much smarter in a plain, narrow belt."

"I'll remember that," I said, "the next time I want to look smart."

Outside, I warmed myself quickly by shoveling the snow clear of the truck's exhaust pipe. Then I shoveled a path forward and started the motor to warm it up. The pickup rocked a little to indicate that Gail was moving around in back. I went back to investigate and found her sitting up with a blanket over her shoulders, pulling on a fresh pair of nylons. The snow was still frozen on the ones she'd had on the night before.

I said, "I told you to stay put."

She made a face at me. "It's not so cold."

Her breath made a misty plume on the still air. Her legs, in those sheer stockings, looked colder than anything on earth. I reached out and pinched one of her toes through the nylon.

"Can you feel that?"

She looked startled. "Why, no, I—"

"You," I said, "are a lovely dope."

I grabbed her by the ankles and pulled her towards me, disregarding her squeals of protest. I gathered her up in my arms, carried her around to the cab and shoved her inside.

"It'll start to get warm as soon as the sun rises, but in the meantime," I said, "you put that coat on and stay in there all covered up if you want to get out of this with a full complement of toes and noses, not to mention fingers and ears. What do they teach you Texas girls, anyway?"

She gave me a grin. "After last night, darling, need you ask?"

I started to close the door and stopped, looking at her. Something had changed in her face. It wasn't just that the hardships of the night had inflicted serious damage on the smooth, hard polish with which she'd embarked on this journey—that her elaborate hairdo was a tousled mess and her careful make-up mostly missing. She didn't even have much lipstick on. Then I realized that it was the mouth itself that had changed. It was softer and prettier than I remembered it.

"What's the matter, darling?" she asked.

"Nothing," he said, "but you'd better comb your hair. You look like a sheep dog."

I went back to melt some snow for coffee on the Coleman stove and told myself that a woman always looks more beautiful after you've made love to her, but I was suddenly a little scared. I didn't want her to turn into a nice girl with a sweet warm mouth. It didn't fit in with my calculations at all.

We had no trouble getting back to the highway, and it didn't take us long after that to reach Carrizozo. For some reason I found myself remembering the time I was working for an Albuquerque newspaper before the war—before Mac got hold of me and taught me a different profession—and had driven through Carrizozo in the spring when the cottonwoods were pale green and the tamarisk hedges were just turning pink. There were no pale new leaves on the cottonwoods today, and no feathery sprays of color on the tamarisks. There were just bare branches and tracked-up snow.

We needed gas, and Gail wanted a nice rest room. When it comes to selecting a place to go to the john, any woman can keep looking much longer than seems natural or safe, and she was no exception. The one she finally picked was no better than the three we'd passed up, as far as I could see, but it sold a brand of gas for which I had a credit card, so I turned in gratefully before she could change her mind.

The man who came up to fill the tank, after setting aside a snow-shovel, was wearing high-laced hunting boots and a red plaid cap with earflaps. He was on the young side of middle age, but not much so, and he had that kind of broad, freckled country face with a long, rubbery, lugubrious mouth and sad light-blue eyes that wouldn't change till he died.

"You folks come far this morning?" he asked. "Have any trouble? No, I reckon you wouldn't in this rig." He patted the fender of the pickup approvingly and glanced up. "Place you want is right around the corner of the building, ma'am, but you'll have to get the key off the cash register inside." He watched Gail walk away, with the veiled expression of a man who has his dreams. Then he glanced quickly at me. "You'll want the regular, I reckon, mister."

"That's right."

He uncapped the tank and brought the hose over. "We get a big snow just about every year," he said, "but damn if people don't act like it was the end of the world every time it happens… You want me to take those chains off for you? You'll beat them to pieces if you leave them on, now the blade's been over the road. Cost you fifty cents."

"It's a deal," I said.

He got a big hydraulic jack and rolled it over. I stood by, waiting. I saw Gail come around the corner of the building, picking her way where the snow was packed so she wouldn't damage her fragile blue pumps. She'd made the necessary cosmetic repairs, combed her hair smooth and hung her pearls back around her neck. Her expensive sweater and skirt were telling no tales. There are still problems to be solved in the fields of science and medicine and international relations, but the ladies' garment industry has got it licked. Nowadays, a girl can spend the night out under quite strenuous circumstances and still greet the morning without a pleat out of place.

She looked pretty and feminine, tiptoeing through the snow like that, but I wasn't watching her just for aesthetic pleasure. I saw her discover the telephone booth nearby—or pretend to discover it. She glanced my way, and I nodded. She made her way over there and picked up the directory without closing the door. Watching her leaf through the pages, I saw her frown quickly and go back a page. She looked up, with a startled expression on her face. I walked over there.

"What's the matter?" I asked.

"It isn't there!"

"No Wigwam?"

"No Wigwam," she said. Then I guess the tone of my voice gave her a belated hint, because she looked up, her gray eyes wide and accusing. "You knew!"

"I knew we wouldn't find it in the phone book," I said.

"How—"

"It was checked two nights ago along with your personal history and various other things."

She frowned as if completely bewildered. "You knew, and still you had us come all this way? You let me—" She stopped, and said naïvely, "You might at least have told me!"

I said, "It was your wild-goose chase, glamor girl. I just came along to watch the show." She gasped, and I said, "Sure, I let you put on your act. It was very good. Congratulations. The double-take, the surprised expression… Anybody'd have thought you really expected to find a place called the Wigwam!" I grimaced. "Now, why don't you just break down, Gail, and tell me what your sister *really* said, and why you went to the trouble of making up this crazy story about an Indian lodge…"

"Excuse me, sir."

The voice came from behind me. Well, I should have known better than to pick a public driveway for the scene, but I was just about through, anyway. I'd done my part to establish the Unbearable Mr. Helm for another day. He'd slipped a little last night; he'd been almost human early this morning, but now he was right back in form. I turned.

"That'll be three-eighty for the gas and fifty cents for taking off the chains, plus tax," the filling station man said. His stolid, freckled face said that quarrels between his customers were none of his business, much as he'd like to know what the hell it was all about. "Oil and water okay. I put your chains in back."

I gave him my credit card. The sound of running footsteps told me Gail was gone; I heard the truck door open and close, hard. I followed the man into the station to sign the ticket.

"There wouldn't be a place called the Wigwam in town?" I asked casually. "A motel or a restaurant or something?"

"There's nothing called the Wigwam, mister, but the Turquoise Motel's a nice place to stay, and if you want something to eat or drink, there's the Cholla Bar and Grill…"

When I got behind the wheel, she was sitting at the other end of the seat, looking straight ahead. I started up the truck and drove away. At the end of town I stopped at the junction where our north-south highway intersected the big paved road going east over the mountains to Roswell in the Pecos Valley, and west over the mountains to Socorro, on the Rio Grande. I turned left and drove out of town. A little way down the road a sign—similar to ones we'd seen while crossing the missile range farther south—warned that the road was occasionally closed for one-and-one-half hour periods during tests. Ahead, the road dipped down into a wide, desolate, snow-covered basin.

"The mountains straight across," I said, "are called the Oscuras, I think. The Army's got a lot of stuff back in there, or did the last time I was through. It's all restricted as hell back in there. Those mountains, just visible, to the south are the Manzanitas."

That got a small reaction from her; she deigned to turn her head and look, but she didn't speak.

"Yes," I said, "that's where the underground test will take place shortly, if it goes off on schedule. It's already been postponed once, and this weather is going to make things rough out there." I paused. "We don't think much of your Wigwam story, Gail, but we're inclined to buy Carrizozo. You can see how it might be the logical place for a drop—that's the jargon for an underground station or post office. It's right where the main highways cross. Anybody going into or coming out of the test area wouldn't need much of an excuse to stop off in Carrizozo to pick up instructions or deliver the goods."

She didn't answer, of course. Her profile was very handsome, but as cold and lifeless as the face on a coin. I drove back and zigzagged through the town, saying nothing. It took three-quarters of an hour, but she finally broke down and spoke.

"May I ask what we are doing?"

I said, "Giving you the benefit of the doubt, glamor girl. I don't think much of that Wigwam story, but I'm willing to be convinced. Now that you've finally come out of your trance, suppose you watch that side of the street while I watch this one. Any sign you can't read, just holler and I'll stop."

She turned at last to look at me directly. "But—"

"So maybe it isn't in the phone book," I said. "And maybe it isn't a motel or restaurant, maybe it's a little curio shop or candy store without a phone. Maybe it's a private residence, with a cute sign out front, only listed under the owner's name."

"But you said—" She paused. "You implied... dreadful things!"

"Gail," I said, "in this business, there's a maxim that goes: suspect everybody once except a woman you've slept with; suspect her twice. You will admit it's odd that there's no such place in the directory, won't you?"

"But you don't really believe—"

"At this stage of the proceedings, I don't believe anything," I said. "I don't disbelieve anything, either. What do you want me to do, take you on faith?"

She flushed slightly, "No, but—"

"Hold it," I said. "We can argue about it later. Look over there."

"What is it?" Her voice was suddenly eager. "Is it—"

"Not what we're looking for, but there are an awful lot of government cars congregating at that motel up ahead. They weren't there the last time we came by... I'll be damned!" I said. "There's Rennenkamp, Old Man Atom himself, the director of the test. I've seen his picture in the paper. Looks like something has got him in a real calm and objective mood as befits a scientist of his age and reputation...

I shouldn't have slowed down, of course. Making a U-turn to avoid passing the place again would have looked too obvious, but I should have driven past rapidly, looking straight ahead, instead of gawking like a tourist at the tall, white-haired old man who was violently haranguing a shorter, darker man in front of a gray car with U.S. GOVERNMENT—INTERAGENCY MOTOR POOL stenciled on the side.

I guess I was curious as to whether the old gent wanted to get started, snow or no snow, and they wouldn't let him, or whether he was telling them he was damned if he was going to risk getting stuck out in the valley today, and to hell with scientific progress and national prestige.

It certainly wouldn't hurt to get some idea as to whether or not the test might be delayed again—but as I came abreast of the place with my bare face showing at the open cab window, a man came out of the motel office and stopped to stare.

"Matt!" he shouted, starting across the sidewalk. "Matt Helm! What the hell are you doing here, you old bastard?"

It was the last question in the world I wanted to be asked in that particular place at that particular time.

14

The funny thing was, I didn't even know him. I mean, I'd have passed him on the street without recognizing him, it had been that long, and even after I remembered who he was, it took me a while to dredge up his name, although I'm supposed to be good at faces and names. But he belonged to that youthful, pre-war period of my life when I'd carried a big 4x5 Speed Graphic camera like a shining sword and worn a press pass in my hat like reporters do in the movies—at least I did until I was laughed out of it by the reporters on the paper, one of whom was this man.

There wasn't anything to do but pull into the driveway and get out and go around to meet him and let him pump my hand enthusiastically. He was one of those ageless, pink, chubby, baby-faced characters who remember everybody they've ever met and are always glad to see them. I don't know why. Personally, I've met a lot of people I'd just as soon forget.

"Well, if it isn't old Flashbulb Helm," he said. "How's

the newspix racket after all these years?"

"I wouldn't know," I said, improvising. "I'm freelancing nowadays." Well, that checked with my original cover as Mr. Helm, photojournalist from California. "What the hell are you doing out here in a snowdrift?" I asked. "I heard you'd gone to Washington to become a political expert or something."

I'd remembered his name then: Frank McKenna, but nobody had ever called him Frank. He'd been universally known as Buddy, and I had no doubt he still was. I remembered Gail, at the window of the truck, and I said, "Honey, this is Buddy McKenna. Don't believe anything he says, even if you read it in the papers."

Buddy gave Gail an appreciative look. "Is that nice?" he asked me reproachfully. He turned to Gail. "Accuracy is the watchword with McKenna, ma'am. I may not get the story, but I'll damn well spell your name right... What did this oaf say your name was?"

I said quickly, "Her name is Gail, and you keep your cotton-picking hands off, old pal, old pal." I looked around. "Just what's going on here, anyway? Isn't that Rennenkamp over there having a hemorrhage about something? Who's the dark-haired guy arguing with him—the intense one with bifocals?"

"That's Naldi, the seismograph man. He can record the rumbling of a hungry stomach through a thousand yards of solid rock. He's been planting his instruments all over these damn mountains; hell, they postponed the party once so he could finish the job. He just drove up to meet us and go in with us—that is, if we do go in. There seems to be some question, weather-wise."

"Who's us, and where's in?"

Buddy hesitated and gave me a sharp glance, but he said readily enough: "Us are noted figures of press, radio and television, selected for integrity and patriotism. It helps if you happen to be a reasonably good reporter, too, but it isn't absolutely necessary as long as you can prove that your grandma never spoke nicely to Karl Marx. Of course, you also have to swear that you won't print a damn thing but what they want you to." He jerked his head towards the tourist court. "In there are also some eminent scientists thawing out their frozen tootsies, some senators and congressmen and some representatives of friendly foreign governments. And if you try to tell me you don't know why we're here, I'll call you a liar."

I grinned. "Of course it's just a guess. I could be wrong."

"Yeah," he said. "Wrong enough to hire a truck and plow through three feet of snow to get here." He paused, but I saw no necessity to put him straight about the ownership of the truck. He went on: "Well, I'm afraid you've had your trouble for nothing, pal, unless you want to grab a candid shot of the old man waving his arms, and that'll probably cost you your camera and a year in jail. The security on this picnic makes the old Manhattan Project look like a national convention with full network coverage."

"Pretty rough, eh?"

"Hell, you can't even throw away a Kleenex you've

blown your nose on without having some snoop pick it up to make sure it contains nothing but snot—no uncensored messages to accomplices on the outside, nothing. They've got a bad case of nerves about something, and this weather isn't making them any happier. We were supposed to land in Alamogordo yesterday and drive up, but the whole damn valley was socked in, so they couldn't put us down any closer than Roswell, and hours late at that. You can imagine—the way the snow was coming down—the fun we had driving in convoy over the mountains in the dark. If the old man wasn't a slave driver at heart, we'd never have made it, but he's bound he's going to set off his big firecracker without any more delay. Naldi's trying to tell him that even after the snow melts those desert roads are going to be too muddy to use, but five gets you ten Rennenkamp won't listen to reason. He's already sore at Naldi for causing one postponement." Buddy frowned, looking past me. "Uh-oh. The little snoop just went to get the big snoop. You'd better get out of here."

"Why?" I asked. "What do you mean?"

"I told you. We've got security with a capital S... Wait a minute." Buddy lowered his voice. "I'm stuck with this junket, and, much as I hate giving a tip away... Look, if you want a story, don't waste your time here. It's all sewed up tight, big Washington deal, no freelancers need apply. Get over to Carlsbad, you know, the Caverns—the National Park—not the town. Check and see if maybe they're not planning to be closed one day very soon.

Nobody's publicizing it, but I've got information that says they will be."

"Meaning," I said, "just what?"

"Use your head. They're closing the caves, kind of casually—for repairs to the stalactites and stalagmites, I guess—so there won't happen to be anybody underground on a certain second of a certain minute of a certain hour of a certain day. They may even clear the personnel from the buildings located directly over the caves, on some excuse or other. Does that ring a bell or doesn't it? Remember, Carlsbad's almost two hundred miles southeast of ground zero, in another range of mountains entirely—if I remember the geography of my home state correctly."

"Wow!" I said. "If you're right—"

"I had it on pretty good authority. Naldi himself advised it, I heard, and he's been studying ground shocks since the last days of Pompeii or thereabouts, so he ought to know what he's talking about. Looks as if somebody isn't quite sure this gun isn't loaded, eh? And little old Buddy's going to be sitting in a lousy little blockhouse out in this lousy valley, looking a mountain full of hot stuff right in the eye... Just get down there, Flash. If anything does go wrong, they'll try to cover up, they always do. I'd like to know there's somebody out here with newspaper training getting the real story of the boo-boo... No, Matt," he said in an entirely different voice, "I'm sorry as hell, but I can't tell you a thing. If you want information, you'll have to apply to the proper... Oh, hello, Peyton."

There were footsteps behind me, and somebody

grabbed my arm and swung me around. There are some beautiful responses to that opening which leave the other fellow much less healthy than he was, but this didn't seem like the proper time to use them. I let myself be turned, and found myself facing a lean Madison Avenue figure in dark-gray flannels, a gabardine topcoat and a hat with a brim so narrow it hardly seemed worth putting on. He didn't look funny, however, not even out here in the land of the broad-brimmed Stetson. No man with those pale fanatic's eyes ever looks funny to me. I saw too many of them goose-stepping in fancy uniforms while I was operating on the continent during the war.

"Is this the man?" he asked.

I thought he was addressing Buddy, and it didn't make sense, but then I saw another man standing by—a bigger, older man who looked uncomfortable in civilian clothes. He might have been ex-Army, but I doubted it. He looked ex-cop to me. He glanced from me to the truck and nodded.

"That's the guy, Mr. Peyton," he said. "That's the pickup he was driving. He was coming along the street real slow with his head out the window like he was looking for something."

"When was this?"

"Oh, say fifteen-twenty minutes ago. When I saw him come by again from a different direction, and stop, I figured I'd better let you know."

The younger man never took his colorless eyes from me. They weren't gray, they weren't blue, and they

certainly weren't green or brown. They must have had
some kind of pigmentation, since they weren't white,
either, but I couldn't put a name to it. They were the eyes
of a man who'd always think he was right, no matter how
wrong he might be.

"Well," he said, "who are you and what have you got
to say for yourself?"

Buddy McKenna stepped forward. "Lay off, Peyton,"
he said. "The boy's just a free-lance photographer looking
for a few pix. Can you blame him? We aren't all on Uncle
Sam's payroll, you know. Some of us have to work for a
living."

It made me feel a little guilty to have him come to my
defense like that, since—although he didn't know it—I
was on Uncle Sam's payroll, too.

The man called Peyton turned slowly to face him.
"Mr. McKenna," he said, "before we started, you were
informed as to the regulations that would be in effect
for this group of observers and the reasons for them.
You were asked not to communicate with anyone from
the time you joined us in Washington for the preliminary
briefing to the conclusion of the experiment when you
would be free to submit your story—subject, of course,
to proper clearance."

"All right, all right," Buddy said, "so who's
communicating? Can't I say hello to an old friend I see
on the street?"

He winked at me. We were newspapermen together,
disrespectfully bamboozling the pompous forces of law,

order and security, as always, for the sake of the picture and the story—and maybe, incidentally, an ancient principle known as the freedom of the press.

"You know this man?" Peyton demanded.

"Sure, I'm just telling you—"

"How long have you know him? When was the last time you were in touch with him?"

"Why, hell, it was…" Buddy thought back and seemed shocked at the passage of time. "Jeez, he was just a long, skinny, green kid with a brand new camera, it must have been a year or two before the war. My God! I didn't think it had been that long!"

"And you haven't seen him since or communicated with him in any way? And today you just *happen* to see him driving along the street… You say he's a photographer? That's very convenient, isn't it, your coming across a photographer friend at just this time? You may be sure the coincidence will be investigated, Mr. McKenna."

Buddy said, "I don't like your insinuations. I didn't send for—"

"In that case," Peyton said coldly, "since you haven't heard from this man in—what is it?—fifteen or twenty years, you're hardly in a position to vouch for him, are you? I think you'd better leave us. I'll talk to you later."

Buddy hesitated, shrugged and gave a mock salute. "So long, Hash. Remember the motto of the working press: *lllegitimati non carborundum.* That means don't let the bastards grind you down."

He strolled away. Peyton watched him go, and I knew

that if anything could happen to Buddy in the way of clearance or censorship troubles, it would. Well, I'd got other men into worse difficulties—LeBaron for one—but I was sorry just the same. On the other hand, while he'd given me some interesting things to think about, Buddy hadn't exactly helped me out, either.

Peyton started to turn back to me, and I braced myself for the coming inquisition, but the top-brass argument by the cars was just breaking up, and he swung his frown in that direction.

The dark-haired man, Naldi, was saying, "Doctor, I respectfully submit that I know these mountain and desert roads better than you do, having explored them quite thoroughly in all kinds of weather—"

"And I say, doctor," Rennenkamp interrupted, "that I am in charge of this operation, and I will not stand for any further delay. If we can harness the energy of the atom and transport mankind to the stars, I find it hard to believe that we cannot solve the problem presented by a few miles of snowy, or muddy, roads."

"Doctor—"

"There will be no further postponement," Rennenkamp said. "That is final, doctor."

The dark-haired man glared at him and flung away, coming towards us briefly so that I could see his face, quite swarthy, with rather small rimless glasses perched on a rather large bony nose. He snatched out a key and started to unlock the door of one of the motel units, and for a moment I caught a view of the back of his head from an angle—the same angle from which I had once viewed the head of a man with black hair through the smoky air of the Club Chihuahua while a girl in a yellow satin dress came teasingly along the edge of the stage…

Then he was gone. I suppose it was my duty to tell Peyton, who was watching the white-haired figure of Dr. Rennenkamp stride firmly across the driveway. I did consider it.

I said, "That was Henry Naldi, wasn't it? The black-haired guy?"

Peyton wheeled to face me. "That was Doctor Alexander Naldi—" He checked himself abruptly.

I grinned. "Alexander," I said. "Thanks. And Rennenkamp's first name—Excuse me, Doctor Rennenkamp's first name is Louis, I believe." I took out my notebook and wrote. "And yours, Mr. Peyton?"

He snatched the notebook from me. It was too bad. He'd put his hand on me once, but I was willing to overlook that, reluctantly. But he wasn't acting at all like a man who wanted help with his little problems, and his problems weren't my problems… Having my notebook, he took me by the arm. Considering the cultivated way he was dressed, he had a very rude way of dealing with people. It was too bad.

"This way, you," he said grimly. "I have some questions for you… Bronkovic, take a look through that vehicle."

"Yes, sir," the big man said. "What about the lady?"

"The lady?"

It must have been a blow to Gail; she wasn't used to

being overlooked. That he hadn't even noticed her face at the cab window showed the dedicated nature of Mr. Peyton; he'd been too busy glowering at the rest of us. He looked now and wasn't particularly impressed. His expression said no pretty face would ever deflect him from his duty by a fraction of a degree.

He started to speak. Then he hesitated, and looked again, and something changed in his pale eyes. He surveyed the truck briefly, as if he hadn't really seen it before. He glanced at the California license plate. He glanced at me. After a moment, he cleared his throat and released my arm.

"On second thought," he said, "on second thought, maybe I've been a little hasty."

For him, that was like an ordinary person's confessing to killing his mother with a stolen axe. I tried not to look surprised, but succeeded only fairly well.

"Yes," Peyton said thoughtfully, "a little hasty. As Mr. McKenna pointed out, you fellows do have a living to make." He handed back my notebook. "I suppose the headlines will read, SCIENTISTS STRANDED IN SNOW. Well, it's legitimate news, and even if it makes us look a little foolish, I see no reason to suppress it. I'm Paul Peyton, security officer in charge. This is Dan Bronkovic, one of my assistants. I'm sorry that I am not permitted to authorize any interview or pictures at this time. You'll have to do the best you can with what you have."

He paused, surveyed us briefly as if committing us to memory, made a gesture towards raising his snappy little hat to Gail and stalked away. Bronkovic, looking puzzled, followed. I walked around the truck and got in and drove away, not fast, but as fast as I could without looking too much like a man with a guilty conscience.

"Well!" Gail said. "What was that? Why did he let us go?"

"I don't know exactly," I said, "but he had our description from somewhere, once he got around to thinking about it, that's obvious. I guess various people in Washington have decided to cooperate after all, and the word's gone out to lay off a tall, skinny man, a beautiful woman and a truck with California plates."

"Oh."

"I must say it's a relief," I said with a grin. "He didn't have what you'd call a reasonable attitude, and he was a little too free with his hands. If he hadn't already had the official word, I might have run into trouble trying to make him listen to my explanation of what I was doing with a loaded revolver and an illicit film capsule in my boot."

I felt a little guilty saying it, now that we were back on a moderately friendly basis again, but there were some things she was better off not knowing—and after all, it wasn't really a lie. I hadn't said there was any film in the capsule.

15

They pulled out a little after eleven. We could see them go from the window of a tourist court near the highway junction. Security or no security, nobody could have missed the caravan of government cars heading out across the valley.

"Well," I said, "I guess there's no doubt about who won the argument. Okay, let's get to work. I didn't want to risk bumping into any of Peyton's minions—no sense pushing our luck—but now they're gone, let's grab some lunch and take this town apart. We'll do it on foot this time, street by street. If you've got anything in the way of boots or overshoes, you'd better put them on. It's getting pretty damn slushy out there…"

It was a rough afternoon, and the snow didn't help a bit. When we weren't wading through the slush, it was being splashed on us by passing cars. At dinner time, the tally stood at no Wigwams, one Tepee, two telephone subscribers named Hogan—a hogan is a Navajo hut—and a small Eskimo igloo constructed by a bunch of Spanish-American kids with happy dark faces. They thought the snow was real great. It had closed the schools for the day.

We checked every name and every structure that could possibly be taken to represent an Indian dwelling of any kind, and finally, at dusk, we stumbled into the Cholla Bar and Grill defeated and so tired that we couldn't even talk until we'd polished off the first round of Martinis.

"I still think," Gail said, "that our best bet is the Tepee."

The Tepee was a tent-shaped drive-in we'd discovered on the edge of town that apparently served ice cream and kindred products in summer.

"It's closed up tight," I said.

"Well, it's just the sort of mistake a... a dying person might make. Tepee-Wigwam. Wigwam-Tepee. Janie was trying to tell me, but she just got confused..."

I said, "Gail, the joint was boarded up. The folks who run the place are in El Paso for the winter. We checked; nobody's been around for months. It's no damn good." She didn't speak, and I said, "You're still quite sure your sister said Wigwam?"

"You keep asking me that. Of course I'm not absolutely sure. There was a lot of noise and... well, she was dying. I've never seen a person die before. But I know what I think I heard. I can't help it if—"

"Okay," I said, cutting her off. "Suppose it is Wigwam, are you quite sure she said Carrizozo?"

She set her glass down so quickly that part of her drink slopped out. "Why don't you say what you really think?" she demanded with sudden violence. "Why don't you say that you still think I… I'm lying, leading you on a wild-goose chase for some… some sinister purpose…!" Her voice broke. "Oh, God, I wish I'd never come on this fantastic expedition! Just look at me! I haven't had my clothes off for two days, and I'm so t-tired and d-dirty I could cry! I wish I'd just told that nasty old b-boss of yours what he could do with his lousy blackmailing… Ouch!"

She leaned down and rubbed her shin where I had kicked her, glaring at me across the tabletop.

"Keep your voice down," I said. "Don't go hysterical on me, glamor girl. Finish your drink and read your menu."

She straightened up. "One of these days," she breathed, "one of these days somebody's going to take a baseball bat to you, and I hope I'm there to see it!"

"Sure," I said. "If you want to pull out, they run buses to El Paso. Either stop screaming at me and behave yourself, or beat it."

There was a little silence, then she pushed a wisp of hair back from her face and picked up her Martini glass. She spoke in a cool voice, devoid of anger or hysteria.

"I thought if I didn't cooperate I'd go to jail as a dangerous enemy agent."

I laughed. "We were bluffing, glamor girl. Haven't you caught on yet? For a poker-playing Texican ranch girl you bluff easier than any human being I ever met. I'd love to play you for money some time. Go ahead and go, wherever you want to. Nothing will happen, nobody will whisper a word against you."

She sipped her drink, studying me over the glass. "Well, I declare," she said slowly. It was the first time she'd really put out with the drawl. "I do declare, it don't seem possible that one man could be so aggravatin' all by himself."

"It's a knack," I said. "I've worked hard at developing it. I'm glad it's appreciated." I hoped she couldn't guess how close this was to the truth.

"I don't understand," she said, dropping the Texas act as suddenly as she'd picked it up. "I don't understand, why are you so anxious to get rid of me all of a sudden? Not that I mind, heaven forbid, but I thought you had some idea you needed me. You certainly went to enough trouble to get me here."

I said, "That was when I thought you might lead me somewhere interesting and profitable. But we've spent a day on it, and nothing's come of it. I haven't any more time to waste." I grinned at her. "Or maybe I'm just turning you loose to see what you do when you think you're not being watched. Take your choice." I let my grin widen in what I hoped was an infuriating way. "Goodbye. It's been real nice, glamor girl. Parts of it, anyway."

She got to her feet, set her glass down very gently, took her coat from a nearby hook and walked out without looking back. Now, I thought, if she had any resources we didn't know about, she'd have to trot them out quick before she lost touch with me altogether. I had another drink and wondered why I was suddenly kind of lonely. I should be satisfied with my own company, shouldn't I, a diabolically clever guy like me?

16

I phoned Mac from a booth by a filling station—the same filling station, as a matter of fact, that we'd patronized when we first arrived. It was the only public phone I knew of in Carrizozo. The same man was sitting at the desk beyond the big window of the building, having a sandwich and a cup of coffee for dinner.

I had no trouble reaching Mac in Washington. "Eric here," I said when he came on the line. "Alexander Naldi. Seismologist, if that's the proper term. Medium height, large head, black hair. Glasses situation confused. He was wearing them today, bifocals yet, but he didn't have them on in Juarez. Maybe he was in disguise, or thought he was."

"I see," Mac said, two thousand miles away. "This is the man from whom Sarah got the films?"

"I wouldn't swear to it in court, but he was in the place at the time, and he's the only person she actually touched while on stage."

"A seismologist, you say?"

"Don't ask me to spell it, sir. A man who studies earth tremors."

"I am aware of the definition of the word."

"Yes, sir. He's all set up to study earth tremors around here. There should be some good ones in a day or two. He seems to be in charge of the earth-tremor department He's also doing his best to stall the project in question. He's responsible for one postponement, and he tried to promote another today, but Rennenkamp wasn't buying."

"I see."

"He has also recommended that the caverns at Carlsbad be evacuated during the test. This conflicts with official reassurances, quoted in the newspapers, to the effect that there isn't the slightest danger to a single precious underground formation."

"You seem to have acquired some fascinating data," Mac said. His voice was cool. "None of it, however, seems to have much bearing on our problem."

"Perhaps not, sir, but—"

"Your job is Gunther. Espionage and sabotage, on whatever scale, are not our concern, Eric. I am sure that in those fields the national interest is being quite adequately safeguarded by the agency or agencies established for the purpose. Never mind Alexander Naldi or the Carlsbad Caverns. You were sent after one man, a man known as Cowboy—"

"Just a minute, sir," I said. If he could split hairs, so could I. "Let's clarify this a bit. Am I looking for Gunther, or am I looking for this Cowboy character?"

"They are one and the same."

"Says who? Everything I learn about Gunther sounds pretty small-caliber to me. Oh, he's involved, sure, up to his neck, but if the Cowboy is their top man locally, it doesn't look to me as if this gigolo is a very likely suspect."

Mac said coldly, "Our assignment, your assignment, Eric, is Gunther. That is the way the orders came through, and that is the way we will execute them." After a moment, he added, "After all, we owe him for LeBaron; he's due for murder anyway. And if they want us to do the detective work, they can so state. In this case they claim positive identification. Do I make myself clear?"

He did. Somebody had reamed him out for interpreting orders loosely or concerning himself with matters outside his jurisdiction, so now we were going to do it by the book. Somebody wanted Gunther. Somebody would get Gunther.

"Yes, sir," I said. "As far as Naldi and the Carlsbad Caverns are concerned, I just mentioned it because I thought you'd want to pass it along."

"That," said Mac sarcastically, "is a strange thought. I will have to pass it along, of course, now that you have presented me with it, but the desire is conspicuously lacking."

I frowned at the glass wall of the booth. He was certainly in a state about something. I said, "I had the impression that everything was sweetness and light and official cooperation, sir."

"What would give you that odd impression?"

I said, "You haven't given our description to any related agencies and asked that we be let alone if encountered?"

"I am not in the habit of circulating the descriptions of our people, Eric, particularly not when they are on secret and potentially dangerous duty."

"Then," I said, "something damn funny is going on around here." I told him what had happened that morning.

"A security officer?" Mac said. "And he'd been told what to look for?"

"Yes, sir. He didn't place me at once, he was too busy acting the Grand Inquisitor the way they do, but when he got around to noticing the lady and the truck and the license plate, he suddenly remembered something and became very gracious indeed."

"I see," Mac said. "I'll investigate. You were careless. That involvement wasn't necessary."

"No, sir. I was scouring the town for wigwams. I didn't expect to run into an official parade like that."

"Considering the date, which I hope you are doing, it's hardly an earthshaking coincidence."

"Earthshaking?" I said. "I think that's a very appropriate word in this connection, sir. Incidentally, there were no wigwams."

"I see." His voice was suddenly soft and sad and far away. "Well, we anticipated that possibility, didn't we? Do your best, Eric. I didn't mean to be… The political situation is a little trying at the moment."

"Yes, sir," I said. "It always is."

"It is hard to explain to people who know nothing about

it that political reliability is not the only qualification necessary for undercover work, or even the primary one."

"They are raising hell about Sarah?"

"Naturally. It always raises hell when an agent defects. I think you had better get me Gunther, Eric. Nobody else has turned up any leads; yours is the only one we have, thin as it is. It should be a smooth, impressive, confidence-inspiring job, preferably one that looks like an accident and embarrasses nobody. Did you receive my little gift?"

"Yes, sir. I am wearing it."

"It is supposed to be an improved model. I would like your comments, later. Just peel off the foil as usual. Do you feel that you are making progress?"

"The preparations are well in hand, sir. I would say she's willing to try anything that'll make life tough for me. All she needs is the chance."

"Let us hope she gets it," Mac said. "I hate to ask a man to offer himself as bait, but—"

"Sure," I said. "Good-bye, sir."

I hung up and stood there for a moment, frowning thoughtfully. A car drove up and a bell rang somewhere on the premises as it crossed a rubber hose lying across the driveway. The filling-station man, in the lighted office, drained his coffee cup and came out. His name was lettered over the door: A.H. (Hank) Wegmann. I assumed it was his name. No one but the owner or manager of the place would put in such long hours.

I opened the door of the booth, paused to let him go by and headed across the lot in the direction of the tourist court a couple of blocks away. He went out to the car by the pumps. It was an Army jeep from some nearby missile outfit, I noticed, with a young enlisted man at the wheel. The idea must have been taking shape in my mind as I walked, but I was almost out of range of the lights before it suddenly graduated from a kind of subconscious nagging to a conscious brain-wave.

It hit me so hard that I almost stopped and looked back to check what I'd seen, but that would have been strictly amateur procedure, and I'd done enough blundering already that day—as Mac had not been slow to point out. I kept walking until the place was out of sight behind me. Then I stopped under a street light and searched myself for something I vaguely remembered shoving into a pocket.

After a little, I found it—the flimsy receipt for the gasoline I had charged that morning. I smoothed out the paper, and there it was again, what had struck me back there: WEGMANN'S ONE-STOP SERVICE, CARRIZOZO, NEW MEXICO. I stood there looking at it, while cataclysmic changes occurred in what I like—though it seems without much justification—to refer to as my brain.

Wegmann, I thought, Wegmann. All day we'd been looking for an Indian tent, and here was Mr. Wegmann. Wigwam—Wegmann. It could have been a coincidence. It could also have been a coincidence that of all the filling stations in town, Gail Hendricks had carefully guided us to this one. She had said, it looked cleaner than the others, and she wanted a nice, clean rest room.

It could be, but I didn't believe it for a minute.

17

Reaching the motel, I paused outside the door briefly, wondering what kind of a scene she'd prepared for me inside. I'd taunted her and sent her away, remember, claiming to have no further use for her. I didn't think she was about to let herself be dismissed in such a cavalier fashion, so it was her move.

I had no more doubts. The only question was whether I was merely dealing with a mortally offended lady pursuing a private revenge, or whether she had other, darker motives. I didn't really think she had, but of course I couldn't rule it out entirely. In any case, it was obvious that I had misjudged her in that El Paso hotel room. Forced to surrender the film capsule under threat of being stripped naked, she'd still managed to hold out on me. She hadn't been nearly as scared as she'd seemed. Questioned about her sister's dying words, she'd come up with the perfect answer. *Wigwam*, she'd said, *the Wigwam in Carrizozo*.

It left her protected. If I already knew about Mr. Wegmann's service station and confronted her with the knowledge, she could claim to have made an honest mistake—the names were that close. If I didn't... well, at least she'd given no more help to the disgusting bully who'd wrecked her dress and threatened to smash her face in. And she could have the satisfaction of imagining me combing Carrizozo for days, searching for a native shelter that didn't exist.

She couldn't have anticipated that she'd be present to watch, although maybe she'd even hoped for that. In any case, given the opportunity to come along—forced to come along, even—she'd made the most of it. I couldn't help grinning wryly as I recalled the way we'd marched around slushy streets for endless hours this afternoon, while she, outwardly cooperative and sympathetic, undoubtedly laughed herself quite sick inside... I turned the knob and went in to see what she'd figured out for me next.

She'd left one small light on, so I'd get the full impact as I came in. That was a flaw, objectively speaking— darkness would have been more suitable to the tragic impression she was trying to convey—and I thought the pathetic, moist, crumpled handkerchief in her trailing hand was overdoing it a little, but on the whole it was a very creditable stage setting. It established the proper mood instantly.

Her fur-lined coat lay on the floor where she'd discarded it, supposedly, as she stumbled forward and flung herself face down on the big bed in tears—too upset by my cruelty, it would appear, to even remove the little plastic boots she'd been wearing over her shoes. A nice touch of verisimilitude was that the boots were muddy.

She gave me plenty of time to appreciate the scene. Then there was an audible gasp as she realized, officially, that she was no longer alone in the room. A moment later she was sitting up, prettily startled and embarrassed.

"Oh! I didn't hear… I must have fallen asleep."

I looked at her for a moment, feeling rather sorry for her. She was pretty good, but she was still an amateur. Sooner or later, she'd get into things she couldn't handle. It wasn't a game, but she didn't know it yet.

I said, "Why, you've been crying! What's the matter, glamor girl. Can't you bear to part from me?"

She stared at me, wide-eyed, and jumped to her feet. "Why, you arrogant, insufferable *beast*—"

She choked and turned away, putting the damp handkerchief to her face. I produced a larger one of my own, fortunately clean. I stepped up and reached around to give it to her from behind.

"Here," I said. "Try a dry one. Wipe and blow."

She hesitated then snatched the cloth without looking around. We stood like that for a little. Then, with a small, tired sigh, she turned and came quite naturally into my arms.

I heard her voice, muffled: "Why do you have to be such a monster? Why couldn't… Why can't I ever fall for a man who's… nice. Just a little nice, just a little…

kind and gentle. I declare, that don't seem like too much to ask."

"Gail," I said. "Gail, I—"

Then, in the direct and clumsy way of the suddenly passionate male, I kissed her thoroughly and reached for the zipper of her skirt. She caught my wrist, but she was smiling now.

"All right," she breathed. "All right, but let's do it properly this time."

"Properly," I said, kissing her again. "It's a hard thing to do, properly, but for you I'll try. I'll be proper as hell."

"Please, darling!" she said, laughing and trying to escape. "I mean, I don't care much for this impromptu sex. Let me take a shower and make myself pretty... I won't be long."

She wasn't, and much later, with darkness in the room, I felt her move beside me in a tentative way. I made no response, breathing evenly. She barely disturbed the bed as she slipped out of it. Apparently the sweater and skirt she'd removed in the bathroom wouldn't do for the next bit, or maybe simple fastidiousness wouldn't let her put them back on after wearing them so long; anyway, she paid a visit to the closet and paused by her suitcase, before she went in there. I heard the muffled click as the door closed behind her. I waited.

For a woman of her looks and background, she was a fast dresser. She was out again in less than five minutes. I was prepared to keep up my impersonation of a man pounding his ear until she was safely gone, but I'd underestimated her again. Instead of sneaking out, she came straight to the bed.

"Matt," she whispered. "Matt, darling."

I grunted, snorted and sat up abruptly. "What—"

I reached for the light switch. The sudden illumination made her blink. She was wearing another sweater, this time a fuzzy tan job with a big loose collar—very dramatic but not much good for keeping the neck warm—and a pair of tapering tan pants. I suppose they're still called pants. They ended short of the ankles and were very, very snug. I looked at them and pursed my lips in a soft whistle.

"Don't be corny, darling," she said. "I'll have you know they're very expensive and very chic. I'm sorry to wake you but I didn't want you to think I... I'd run away, or anything."

"Where are you going?"

She shook her head mysteriously. "I'm not going to tell you. It's just an idea—"

"Little Gail, girl detective," I said sourly. "Look, glamor girl, don't you realize that a couple of people have already been killed very dead? If you've got an idea, tell me about it, and we'll figure out what to do about it together."

She shook her head again. "No, I want to do this myself. You said some things that weren't very nice this morning, remember? You acted as if you thought I... Anyway, I want to try. Maybe I can help."

I hesitated, and said sulkily, "All right, be the expert.

Get yourself killed. Why bother to wake me up to tell me?"

"Oh, Matt!" she said, in a hurt little-girl voice. I didn't say anything. She started to speak again, changed her mind and turned towards the door.

I said, "Gail." She looked back. I reached down into one of my boots lying by the bed and came up with my .38 Special revolver. "Here, damn it," I said. "Do you know how to use it?"

"Well, I've shot them—"

"Okay," I said. "It's loaded. It kicks like a mule. Try not to blow your fool head off. Now get the hell out of here and let me sleep."

I watched the door close behind her. A diligent detective type would, I suppose, have hauled on his pants and followed, but I just let her go. The risk of being caught tailing her was too great; besides, I didn't figure she was going very far, just to the filling station a couple of blocks away, where Mr. Wegmann would, no doubt, be very glad to see her.

18

I don't apologize for going to sleep; there wasn't anything
else to do, and it might have been a long time before I
got another chance. When the knock came at the door,
it took me a moment to realize what it was and where I
was. It was a soft little knock, the kind of diffident knock
a woman might use who'd forgotten to take the key and
hoped she wasn't going to have to wake anybody up to
get herself let back in.

Well, that was all right, and as a matter of fact I hadn't
seen her take a key, but we have a routine that covers
doors and the opening thereof in the middle of the night
when the situation warrants a red-alert rating. I made
some kind of a sleepy sound to let her know I was coming
and she didn't need to break it down. I sat up and put
my feet into my boots—people have sustained painfully
smashed toes, opening doors barefooted. I looked around
the darkened room, placing the furniture in my mind so
I wouldn't have to look again. Then I got up and stole

silently to the door and yanked it open from a certain angle in a certain way, stepping aside quickly.

The first man in was easy. He must have been braced against the door, ready to shove it open hard to throw me off balance. He came hurtling past me like an Army fullback getting up steam to hit the Navy line on a bright fall day along the Hudson. I merely had to stick out my booted foot innocently and he spilled headlong. I made a note of the fact that he seemed to be armed, and it therefore wouldn't do to leave him unattended too long, but it was time to deal with Number Two, who was bigger and cagier.

He had a gun, too, but I kicked it out of his hand— which was a mistake. It's always a mistake to kick at a high target, even with the best kicking technique in the world, unless you know the man opposing you is a fool, or expect the kick to be immediately disabling. Well, the real karate and savate experts can get away with it, maybe, but I'm not in that class.

I knew I was exposing myself to retaliation the instant my knee straightened beyond a certain point, and I was letting myself fall backwards towards a clear space in the room even as he made the standard response of grabbing my foot and dumping me on the back of my head. He scored the point, but I got my foot out of hock, hit the floor in a back somersault and was up again before he could reach me.

There was a groan off to the side. I knew where Number One had landed. He'd rammed the bed with his head as he pitched forward, which was a step in the right direction, but I thought I'd better do something more permanent about him while Number Two was still taking things easy and sizing me up. I jumped up on the double bed. The big one couldn't figure out what I wanted up there, and he wasn't in a hurry to find out. He came forward slowly, alert for a trick.

Finally, he lunged for me. I vaulted to one side, dropping over the foot of the bed and landing on his partner, driving the boots in hard. It wasn't a very nice thing to do, but I wasn't feeling very nice. A girl had made love to me, smiled at me, and gone out to sell me to the highest bidder. Even if it was what I'd expected and worked for, it didn't make me very happy.

I jumped on the first guy hard and threw myself away from the reaching arms of Number Two. That was enough of the Douglas Fairbanks routine. I'm not really that young or that acrobatic except when I have to be. Number One was safely out of it now; he was due in the shop for body work and engine repairs. But his big *compadre* was still coming after me like a great bear, only after that first neat, foot-twisting throw I wasn't kidding myself: this bear knew unarmed combat.

The fact is that all this karate-judo stuff is really effective only on people who don't know how. Sure, I'm acquainted with a lot of bare-handed ways of knocking out or even killing an unskilled man, or one who isn't aware that mayhem is coming his way. But when the other guy is hep and ready, then everybody's got trouble, and the best thing to do, particularly if he's bigger than you, or if you can't find yourself something to chop, stab, or shoot with, is to depart the joint and take to the hills.

The trouble was, I was in pajamas, he was between me and the half-closed door and while the motel carpet was downright littered with firearms—well, two—a feint towards the nearest one showed me that the big fellow was just as aware of them as I was. If I wanted a gun, I was going to have to fight him for it, and that was just what I was trying to avoid. We don't do this stuff for fun, you know, or even for exercise. Some people do try to play at it, but it's not really a sport, like boxing or wrestling. Basically, it's for keeps.

He was one hell of a big guy, towering square and black against the dim illumination of the door and window—a mountain of a man without a face. He made me feel spindly and fragile for all my two hundred pounds and six feet four. Maybe I had the reach on him by a little, but it didn't cheer me up remarkably. I didn't really want to reach him—with anything less than an axe.

Then we were mixing it, if you could call it that. What it amounted to was that he'd try something in a careful and experimental way, and I'd catch the shadowy movement and show him that I knew the answer, and he'd cover up quickly. Then I'd trot out one of my pet tricks, and he'd let me know he'd read that book, too. Two guys who know the stuff don't take any chances with each other, and it's very dull to watch.

That is, it's dull if you don't happen to be one of the

guys. I knew that lightning would strike the instant I made a mistake or let myself get trapped in a corner or tangled in the furniture. As we shuffled around each other warily in the dark room, the thought of Gail returned to my mind. It wasn't anything to be bitter about, I told myself. It was what we'd wanted, Mac and I, wasn't it? I remembered Mac's words: *You can't trust her, but untrustworthy people can sometimes be very useful...*

I woke up suddenly to the fact that I was spoiling my own game by being so hard to take. After all, clear back in El Paso, we'd planned for her to sell me out, and here I was doing my best to queer the sale. I turned and kicked the unconscious man lying nearby right in his dim white face.

The big one spoke for the first time. "Why," he growled, "you lousy bastard, kicking a man who's down!"

Then, enraged, he charged as I'd hoped he would, with that provocation. He forgot all the nice scientific blows he knew that would kill me or cripple me for life. He charged like a giant grizzly, and I hit him once feebly to make it look good and let him sweep me up in his arms. I don't believe there's a case on record where one man has actually managed to squash another full-grown healthy man with that bear hug. Even breaking an opponent's back from that position isn't easy to do. At least so I'd been told, but as the arms closed about me I started wondering about the accuracy of my information.

I fought back, of course, as I'd be expected to do, frantically. I tried for the groin, but he knew that one, so I tried for the eyes, but I couldn't reach them. He had me pretty well tied up, and he was increasing the pressure, growling deep in his throat. I realized abruptly that if he'd ever received any orders about taking me alive—which I was counting on—he'd forgotten all about them.

I'd miscalculated his loyalty to his partner, and I was in serious trouble. The room was getting darker, and I said the hell with it and went limp as a last resort, beating real unconsciousness by only a little. This didn't bring any marked improvement in the situation. I wasn't breathing much any more, and the station was just about to go off the air when there was a small chopping sound somewhere and the pressures surrounding me eased perceptibly.

The sound came again, accompanied by a little breathless whimpering noise. The arms holding me let go abruptly, and I stumbled back, grabbing a chair to keep from falling. The room was still too dark and my focus wasn't good, but I saw the big man who had almost killed me go to his knees, shielding his head with his arms, while over him hovered a slender, breathless figure in tight light pants and a fuzzy sweater…

I managed the breath I needed and stumbled forward. She had him helpless on all fours now and was systematically hacking away at his head with the butt of the gun I had given her—as if intent on hammering him right through the floor. I came up behind her and caught her arm. She whirled.

"Easy," I said. "Easy, Gail."

"Oh!" She looked down at the gun she was holding wrong-end-to and threw it on the bed. She controlled her breathing with a great effort and spoke flatly. "I thought he'd killed you. Are you all right?"

"Well, I'm not dead," I said. "Thanks."

She swayed and put out a hand to steady herself. I caught her and held her. I would like to be able to report that my only emotions at that moment were love and gratitude—and remorse for having misjudged her—but the picture wasn't that clear in my mind. My ribs ached and my back hurt and oxygen deliveries to my lungs were far behind schedule. It was hard to concentrate on the woman in my arms, but I was aware that she was trembling.

"My dear man," she breathed, "my dear, dear man! Did you know you had the power to transform a female clothes-horse into a raging tigress? I've never in my life done anything like that before." Then she stiffened against me, looking past me. "Matt!" she breathed. "Matt, look!"

I released her and turned. The big man had slumped over on his side. A shaft of light from the open door struck him squarely as he lay there, and I saw his face clearly for the first time. Blood from his lacerated scalp had run across it, but I could see it was the face of Dan Bronkovic, the ex-cop Mr. Paul Peyton, security officer, had introduced as his assistant.

I drew a long breath, feeling a little dizzy. I walked over to the other man who was lying by the foot of the bed and bent down. His face was in worse shape than Bronkovic's, but it was undoubtedly the face of Peyton himself. I don't suppose it was nice to laugh. Maybe I was just a bit hysterical.

19

Gail came in from the bathroom, drying her hands with a face towel. She stopped just inside the room, startled.

"Matt! What are you doing?"

I finished giving the injection to Bronkovic, who was showing signs of reviving, and went over to squirt a dose into Peyton, who might have remained passive without it—he wasn't in very good condition—but there wasn't any sense in taking chances. I got up and cleaned off the hypo with the stuff provided in the little kit we're all issued, packed everything neatly back the way it was supposed to be and tucked the kit behind the lining of my suitcase. I turned to face Gail, who was standing there looking at me shocked and accusingly.

"Look, glamor girl," I said, "this isn't TV. In real life you don't go to all the trouble of knocking people out just to have them wake up and raise hell at the critical moment. Now I can be sure they'll both sleep till morning."

"But—" She licked her lips. "But they're hurt! They

need a doctor! They should be in the hospital!"

That's the trouble with amateurs: they're inconsistent. A few minutes ago she'd been trying to beat the guy's brains out, and now she was worrying about his health.

"Look—" I said as the telephone rang.

Gail glanced at me quickly. I went over to pick up the instrument as it jangled again.

"Yes?" I said.

"This is the manager," a deep female voice said. "Is everything all right in there?"

"Certainly," I said. "Why shouldn't everything be all right?"

"We've had a complaint, sir, from one of the neighboring rooms about a disturbance—"

I hesitated, wondering whether to pretend that we'd been having a drunken argument, or just looking for a lost collar button. But there's no percentage in putting on an act when you don't have to. It was time to call in the brass and let them fight it out, anyway.

I asked curtly, "What's your name?"

"What… Why, I'm Mrs. Meadows. I own this place; that is, my husband and I own it."

"Where's your husband?"

Her voice said bitterly, "Where is he always? If you find out, let me know. Or don't bother. I'm not that interested any longer."

"I see," I said. "Well, Mrs. Meadows, as a matter of fact everything is not all right, and I'd like you to get me Washington, D.C. The number is…"

I gave her the number, or one of them. She hesitated. "I... There's not going to be any trouble, is there? I mean—"

"I'm trying to avoid trouble and publicity, Mrs. Meadows."

"But how do I know... I mean, who are you?"

In my next incarnation, I decided, I'd pick a world that wasn't populated by smart and suspicious women. I said, "You can listen in through your switchboard, can't you?"

"I assure you, sir," she said stiffly, "I never listen to private calls."

"Well, listen to this one," I said. "It's all right, as long as you don't gossip about what you hear. After I've finished talking to my chief in Washington, you can ask him any questions you like. Now put my call through, please."

I identified myself to the girl in the Washington office in a way that let her know there was not only a witness in the room from which I was speaking, there was also an ear on the wire. She'd pass the word to Mac. A minute later I heard his voice.

"Yes?"

"This is Matt, sir," I said. The fact that I didn't use my code name was a further warning.

"Yes, Matt?" he said. The repetition of the name meant he was reading my signals loud and clear.

"Calling from Carrizozo, New Mexico," I said. "Room 14, Turquoise Motel, Mrs. Meadows, manager. Mrs. Meadows is listening and would like identification and reassurance when we've finished talking."

"Very well."

"First, you were to submit some information concerning a certain scientific gentleman, a specialist in vibrations. How was it received?"

"Not well," he said dryly. "I was informed that the matter was well in hand, and that we should mind our own business. As for the gentleman in question, he's supposed to be a good man who's been working a little too hard. That is the word for publication."

So that was the dope on Naldi. Publicly he was supposed to be showing symptoms of overwork; privately he was being watched, and it was none of our damn business.

"That brings us," I said, "to the description of two people and a vehicle that had received unexpected circulation locally. You were going to investigate, remember?"

"I remember. The investigation was fruitless." His voice was grim. "It is the same department that refused us access to its records recently. We will receive no cooperation from that quarter."

"Don't be too sure, sir," I said. "Give them a ring and tell them I've got two of their boys here and would like them hauled away. I think they'll cooperate to that extent."

There was a little pause. Mac spoke softly, far away. "Was that necessary?"

"Not at all, sir," I said. "I could easily have stood still and let them shoot me full of bullet holes. They had the equipment and, as far as I could make out, the desire. There wasn't much time to investigate motives, and the room was dark."

"Give me an idea of the approximate extent of the damage."

"One lacerated scalp and probable concussion," I said. "Fracture unlikely but possible. One set of badly damaged ribs with probable internal injuries. Some plastic surgery may be required on this one. Both have received Injection C and are sleeping peacefully."

"There was no warning?"

"No preliminary conversation whatever. When I opened the door, it was as if I'd dynamited Boulder Dam. They poured all over me."

"You have no idea what they wanted?"

"No, sir. Maybe you can find out from the other end."

"Maybe. You can be certain I will try. Are you all right?"

"It's kind of you to ask, sir," I said. "It was close, but I had help. I'm fine."

"How much time do you want?"

"Half an hour ought to do it. Better not make it much longer. We'd hate to lose either of them, wouldn't we? And see if you can straighten things out so I don't fall over any more of them, sir. It confuses the issue badly."

"I'll endeavor to do that," he said grimly, and I thought there might be some activity in Washington in the near future. "Now let me speak to Mrs. Meadows," he said. "Mrs. Meadows, now that you have heard this conversation, I advise you to forget it. Somebody will call on you shortly with credentials I think you will find adequate…"

I laid the phone down and looked at Gail. "Well, now you know how it's done," I said. "If you're wondering why we let the lady listen in, that's psychology. If we'd kept her off the line—if we could have—she'd have been curious and suspicious. Since she was allowed to listen to important government secrets, she may be proud and scared enough to keep her mouth shut... What's the matter?"

She was watching me in a preoccupied way, frowning a little. "Injection C," she said. "Does that mean there are Injections A and B, too?"

"Don't be nosy," I said. "But since you ask, A is permanent and very quick, but leaves traces. B is slower but can't be detected in the body after a short time—it can pass for heart failure if you set it up right. One that's both instantaneous and undetectable is in the works. Does that answer your question?"

She shivered slightly. "I'm sorry I asked. You're not... not a very nice person, are you, Matt?"

"I'm terrible," I said, "but you've known that since El Paso, so let's just pass up the subject of me and how awful I am. Right now I'd like to know how you made out. We haven't got much time; we want to be out of here before the rescue squad arrives."

She was looking at me blankly. "How I made out?"

"You went on a mission, remember? A secret, mysterious mission. Something you didn't want to tell me about; you wanted to do it by yourself. You wanted to help."

There was a little silence, and something in the room seemed to change. Something went out of it suddenly, something that had been warm and friendly and kind of nice. She went phony on me is the best way I can describe it.

"Heavens, I'd completely forgotten!" she gasped. "Coming in and seeing you fighting like that just drove it plumb out of my mind... Matt, darling, I've got it!"

"Got what?"

"Don't be silly, what we've been looking for, of course! Darling, I've found it! I started thinking about what you'd said. You know, you asked me if I was quite sure Janie had really said Wigwam, and I said I was, almost. And then you asked if I was quite sure she'd said Carrizozo. Well, the more I thought about it... Anyway, I went out to look at the map in the truck, and I made a couple of phone calls. Matt, do you know a town called Ruidoso?"

"Sure," I said. "It's about thirty-five miles from here, up in the mountains on the other side of Sierra Blanca, the big peak we passed on the way up. Horse races are run there in the summer. Ruidoso Downs. The village of Ruidoso itself is just up the canyon from the track." I frowned. "What about Ruidoso?"

"Darling, you're being downright stupid! Don't you see? Carrizozo-Ruidoso. *That's* where I made my mistake. They sound alike, and I'd never heard of Ruidoso and I'd heard of this place, so... Don't you understand?"

I said, watching her, "I thought, all Texans knew about Ruidoso Downs. Certainly enough of them go there for the races."

Her eyes narrowed. "I declare, you're acting very strangely. I thought you'd be proud of me! Don't you understand, I've got it, I've got your lousy wigwam! The Wigwam Lodge in Ruidoso!"

20

There wasn't much conversation during the first part of the journey. I didn't know what her thoughts were, and I didn't want to look at her to find out.

As for my own thoughts, they were confused. She'd saved my life, was the thing I kept remembering, and still, instinct warned me she was being much less than honest with me now. It disturbed me to be heading towards Ruidoso, far back up in the high mountains on the wrong side of the valley, as far as the atom test was concerned. But then, Mac had said that atomic explosions were really none of my business. Gunther was. He could as easily be in Ruidoso as elsewhere. Or the woman beside me could be leading me around by the nose for laughs, but she was still the only lead we had. I had no choice but to stick with her.

Presently she glanced at me. "I thought you said it was only thirty-five miles."

I said, "That's the direct road across the mountains.

Most of it's unpaved, and it's probably all knee deep in snow. I thought we'd better stay on the pavement. It's longer but surer."

"Of course." After a while, she said, "Matt."

"Yes?"

"You're going to kill him, aren't you?"

"Sam Gunther?" I said. "The Cowboy? Yes, if I can find him. That's my job." Her silence had an accusing quality, and I said quickly, "I told you from the start that if we were successful in our mission, Sam wasn't likely to survive it very long."

"Yes, but I didn't know…" She shivered. "I didn't dream… Not until I saw the way you acted with those men, with that hypodermic."

There was a little silence. I shifted gears as the road steepened and we climbed upwards through the pines.

"It's all… rather shocking," she said. "I didn't know things like this went on, darling. I didn't know people like you existed." She hesitated. "I suppose I should be horrified. Maybe I am. Don't expect too much of me. Just tell me what you want me to do…"

It was a nice touch, a nice offer. I would have liked to think it was sincere. I told her something, hoping it sounded sensible and plausible.

Soon we were over the top of the pass, rolling down the other side towards Ruidoso. Something had been done to the highway since I'd last seen it, but no one had figured out a way to keep the snow from falling on it—or if someone had it didn't work. It took me a while to find my way through the maze of dirty white mounds and ridges thrown up by shovels and plows at the fancy intersection. Finally I reached the town itself, which is up a side canyon.

Here also changes had been made, for better or worse, depending on whether or not you like your mountain villages modernized. We drove up the main street. There was a good deal of snow and not much light.

Gail licked her lips. "I don't think I'll ever drive down a strange street again without looking for a sign saying— There it is." Her voice didn't change as she said it.

The buildings themselves were a little off the main street, down in a hollow of pines, but the sign was right at the sidewalk: WIGWAM LODGE. I turned into the driveway and parked the truck with half a dozen other vehicles, most of which had ski racks—some complete with skis—on the roof. Well, it was good weather for it. I got out and walked around to let Gail out, although the chivalrous gesture seemed wasted on the leggy, boyish figure that emerged.

I steadied her as she slipped on the hard-packed snow. There was no wind at this hour of the morning, and it was very silent under the pines. We might have been miles from civilization, instead of a mere thirty yards from the little town's main street.

"Easy," I said. "Don't break a leg now."

She said, "Matt, I'm scared. And cold."

I took my little gun out of my pocket. "Here," I said, "it's still loaded. Don't shoot yourself and try not to shoot me, please, but don't hesitate to use it if you have to. If somebody's got to be dead, we'd rather it wasn't us. Well, I don't have to tell you. You've done all right with it so far."

"What—what do you think will happen?"

"I don't know, but they've already taken one crack at us, up in San Agustin Pass, remember? There's no doubt that they know us. Well, if they come to us, it'll save our looking for them."

She was looking at the little revolver. "Matt, I... Hadn't you better keep it?"

"Go on, take it. I've got a couple more, courtesy of some sick friends. We're gun-heavy, glamor girl. An armored division would have to be called out to match our firepower."

She took the little five-shot revolver, tucked it into the top of her pants and smoothed the bulky sweater over it. I looked at her and tried to remember the moment I'd fallen in love with her, but you never know it when it happens. I studied her face, not forgetting that we'd made love, or that she had saved my life, or that there actually was a Wigwam Lodge in Ruidoso, even though there was— or used to be—a gent named Wegmann in Carrizozo... I tried to sort out the valid evidence from the possible coincidences, making allowances for my own suspicious nature, and got absolutely nowhere. I didn't know.

It was a hell of a time to be standing around in the snow feeling mushy and sentimental about a woman who could be leading me into a trap—who had to lead me into a trap, if I was to do the job I'd come here for. I reached out quickly and did something I'd been wanting to do ever since that style of garment came on the market. She jumped a foot.

"Ouch!"

"Come on," I said. "Let's see what's inside."

I started for the lighted door of the lodge. She came along, reaching back to rub the injured spot. "That isn't funny," she said with dignity. "Besides, it's vulgar. Besides, it hurts."

"If your bottom were decently attired, my dear," I said, "it wouldn't get pinched… Well, here we are." The skinny blonde kid who opened the door was wearing a quilted robe and flannel pajamas, looked kind of cute even though her hair was in curlers. She called her mother, a stout blonde lady, who arrived in a flannel robe and nightgown. Her hair was in curlers, too, but she'd forgotten how to look cute years ago.

We transacted business at a desk in the big rustic lobby that was littered with ski equipment and had the strange, specialized, incomprehensible atmosphere of a place devoted to a sport you're not the least bit interested in at the moment. There have been times when the idea of sliding down a hill on a pair of boards seemed very attractive—I've done my share of it—but this just wasn't one of the times.

"I didn't know you had a ski area here," I said to the woman.

"Oh, we've had a little one for years, sir," she said, "but now they're opening a big one up on Sierra Blanca—that's the big white mountain to the north. Well, I guess everything's white today, haha, but it stays white all winter. Here's your key. You're in Cherokee, the third cabin around to the right. The stove's turned on and there are extra blankets in the closet. I hope you don't mind finding your own way. My daughter has a bad cold, and I—"

"That's all right," I said. "We'll find it. Cherokee."

"I hope you'll be comfortable, sir. We serve breakfast in the dining room from six-thirty…"

I went back across the yard for the suitcases. Gail fell into step beside me as I returned, and we walked together along a shoveled path around the main lodge. After passing a log cabin named Arapahoe and one called Blackfoot, we came to Cherokee. I set the suitcases down, got the key from my pocket and opened the door. It was dark inside. Warm air flowed out to meet me as I picked up the suitcases again and stepped forward.

The lights came on abruptly, and I saw two men facing me. I had seen them both before: Wegmann and Naldi. As I drew back instinctively, a hard object poked me in the back.

"Don't move!" It was Gail's voice, breathless and kind of pleading. "I'm sorry, but *please* don't move, darling."

Somebody saved me the trouble of making up my mind by stepping out of the nearby bushes and laying a gun-barrel or a sap alongside my head.

21

When things cleared up again, I was lying on the floor inside the cabin. The door was closed. At least I could feel no cold draft. I was aware that the borrowed firearms—the ones I'd been careful to mention to Gail—had been removed from my possession—which was perfectly all right. I'd never looked upon this as a gun job, anyway. I'd only brought the weapons along as props, to establish my character as a dangerous man bent on a deadly mission. It wouldn't do for anybody to think I'd come here wanting to be hit over the head.

Despite a throbbing headache, lying there with my eyes closed, I felt kind of happy and peaceful. I suppose, as the victim of cold-blooded treachery, I should have been angry, but hell, I'd practically conned the girl into it, hadn't I? Now that it had actually happened, I couldn't develop any strong resentment. It was what we, Mac and I, had planned from the start, wasn't it? There remained only the question of whether or not she had betrayed me into the right hands.

Her voice reached me from some distance: "You didn't have to hit him! He wasn't doing anything! You promised—"

A man's voice, closer, said, "I was just making sure. After all, you said he was a dangerous—a trained government man sent to get me. They must think I'm real important." The man laughed as he stepped closer and kicked me casually in the side. "He don't look very dangerous lying there."

"Stop it, Sam!" Her voice was cold. "We made a deal. I've kept my part, now you keep yours. Go buy a football if you have to kick something."

Well, there was my answer. It had been a long, long chance, but it had worked. *I think you had better get me Gunther,* Mac had said, and here he was. All I had to do, now, was get him. I opened my eyes.

He was still the movie cowboy in boots, stagged pants and a big light hat. Tonight he was wearing one of those straight, sawed-off saddle-length overcoats that are often worn by ranchers and people who like to be taken for ranchers. In the background, I could see Wegmann, the service-station man, with his freckled country face. He was holding a gun. Dr. Naldi, the seismologist, was also there wearing his bifocals, but unarmed. It seemed like an odd assortment of conspirators, but then, they usually are.

"Up, you!" Gunther said. I got to my feet unsteadily. "All right!" he snapped. "Where are they? We know you've got them!"

Wegmann said impatiently, "I still say this is a waste

of time. My men have already lined up the equipment, visually. The map and other data Dr. Naldi claims to have copied would have been very useful if delivered in time, but they are no longer necessary."

"Claims to have—" This was Naldi speaking hotly. "I did copy them, and if you had let me deliver the films to you in Carrizozo, instead of—"

"Dr. Naldi, you may be an expert on earthquakes, but you know very little about undercover work." Wegmann's voice and attitude had changed somewhat since he'd sold me gas in Carrizozo. "Your contact in Juarez was Gunther. This was agreed on. For obvious reasons, we could not have your part of the operation connected with mine in any direct way; that was an elementary precaution. As I explained to you when we first made our arrangements, the impression we wished to give, if anything went wrong at your end, was that of simple espionage with the information being smuggled straight out of the country. If everything looked perfectly safe, Gunther could then transmit the films back north for us to use. If it didn't... Well, it didn't, so we've had to get along without your valuable contribution, doctor. It slipped out of our hands. You should have retained a copy—it would have been easy enough to make—but you didn't. You very clumsily got yourself suspected, and your information intercepted. It makes one wonder if you really managed to copy the correct documents, and if so whether the photographs were in focus and properly exposed. In any case, it does not matter now."

"It certainly does matter!" Naldi's face was white. "To obtain those pictures, I risked my career and my reputation. Risked? As it had turned out, I sacrificed them! And now you try to minimize... I will show you whether I copied the right documents or not!" He turned his head. "Gunther!"

Gunther nodded and turned to me. "All right, where are those films? We know you've got them. She told me you brought them along to trap me in some clever, clever way." I shook my head. He grinned at me, pleased. He wouldn't have liked it if I'd made it easy. "Well, we'll just have to do it the hard way, then," he said. "Strip."

I didn't look directly at Gail, but I could see that she was smiling oddly. I sat down on a chair to pull off my boots. Gunther took them and gave them to Naldi who, squinting through his bifocals, examined them carefully. I got up and passed my coat and shirt over for inspection. I dropped my pants and kicked them over. It wasn't fun, exactly, but when you've been searched as often as I have, you come to take it with reasonable equanimity, even in mixed company.

As I straightened up, wearing nothing but socks, shorts and T-shirt, I saw Gail looking me over with a strange kind of intentness.

"All the way!" she murmured. I remembered a nightclub in Juarez and a hotel room in El Paso. "All the way, darling! Take it off!"

All of them were busy going through my clothes—except Wegmann, who was handling the gun department with professional concentration. I watched Gail come up to me deliberately.

"Remember, Matt, darling?" she murmured.

"How could I forget?" I said. "You bring it back so clearly."

"You laughed at me," she said. "You ripped my lovely dress off and thought I looked very funny standing there in my furs and… and my foundation garment, like a cheap, leggy pin-up. I promised myself right then that you'd pay for it, no matter what it cost me! I—I had to keep that promise. I couldn't forget it just because."

She stopped. "They won't hurt you," she said after a moment. "That was part of the deal."

"Sure."

She looked me over once more, unsmiling now, but she'd paid for the privilege and she was going to by-God use it. "Dr. Naldi," she said without turning her head, "I think—I just remembered something. Something he said once. You'd better look at those boots again, closely." She spoke to me. "Matt."

"Yes?"

"I *had* to do it. Do you understand? I—I'm a proud woman; I can't bear to be made to look ridiculous."

"Sure." I glanced towards Naldi who was about to do a dissecting job on my boots with a pocket knife. "Never mind the knife," I said. "No sense wrecking a good pair of boots. What you need is a screwdriver. Take off the right heel."

Gail smiled. I guess she was remembering herself

saying, under very similar circumstances: *Well, I don't see much point in putting up a losing battle for my girdle and bra.* The past was very strongly with us as we stood there facing each other—the few days of past we'd shared.

"Sarah said Wegmann, didn't she?" I said. "That's the guy over there with the gun, the gas-and-oil man? And you went to the filling station and made your deal. That's where you disappeared to, isn't it?"

She nodded. "I didn't expect to find Dr. Naldi and Sam there, of course. They were hiding in a storage room with a lot of tires and stuff. They had barely escaped some kind of general security roundup. I guess the men who came to get you at the motel were part of it. We worked it out together. It was Dr. Naldi's idea that there was bound to be some place called Wigwam somewhere up in this locality with all the motels and summer places, and that Ruidoso does sound very much like Carrizozo if you say it fast."

"In this locality?" I said. "What's so important about this locality? The project they're interested in is clear across the valley."

She shook her head to indicate that she didn't know. There was a sound of triumph from Naldi. He had the boot heel off and was shaking the little capsule out of the hollow space inside. I looked at Gail standing before me soberly, not triumphant but not remorseful, either.

"You take your vengeance seriously, glamor girl," I said. "It must have cost you something to deal with Gunther, the man who made a renegade of your sister and probably had her killed."

"You're only saying that!" she retorted. "I asked your chief who killed her—remember?—and why. He didn't know." She didn't want to believe it, I saw; it would be inconvenient. "You haven't any proof! Anyway, no matter what Sam's done, what you're after is murder, just plain, brutal murder, you can't deny that! I don't feel much guilt for interfering, if that's what you're driving at."

"And what about the other thing you're interfering with?" I asked, with a gesture towards Naldi and Wegmann. "I don't know exactly what they have in mind, but the general idea seems to be that they're going to try, somehow, to sabotage an important government project. What about the help you're giving them?"

She laughed shortly. "Frankly, darling," she said, "those atom bombs always did give me the creeps, and I don't blame anybody for being upset about them and trying to stop them. The hell with whether or not it helps the Russians. All that fall-out poisoning the very air we breathe—"

"Very dramatic," I said, "but you ought to check your facts. It just so happens that there's no fall-out or atmospheric contamination from an underground burst."

"Well, there's something else," she said. "Dr. Naldi says—" She paused, as if slightly embarrassed.

"What does Naldi say?"

"Well, it sounds kind of farfetched, I'll admit. Something about continuing harmonic vibrations set up by the recent Russian tests that have caused a massive instability—I think he said massive instability—like when a regiment of soldiers walk in step across a bridge. They can make the birdge start to swing and eventually wreck it."

I said, "You wouldn't know a massive instability if one came walking down the street, Gail."

"Well, Naldi would, and he says there's danger, real danger, if this test is allowed to proceed before the amplitude of the induced waves has diminished below the critical… Well, anyway, I think that's what he said. He was talking pretty fast, and I didn't understand all the long words."

"Sure," I said. "Danger of what?"

"Why," she said, "of earthquakes, naturally! Worldwide earthquakes!"

I stared at her and started to laugh, but a hand on my shoulder swung me around abruptly. It was Gunther, of course; he was another one of those who can't keep his fingers to himself. Dr. Naldi was there, too, his face grim and angry—Wegmann had moved in a little with his gun.

"Where is it?" Gunther demanded.

"Where's what?" I asked innocently.

Dr. Naldi thrust the empty halves of the capsule under my nose. "Where are the films, Mr. Helm?"

I had a choice to make. I could tell them the films were in Washington, but they might believe me. If they did, having no further use for me, they might shoot me through the head or simply tie me up and leave me there. So I smiled mysteriously, shook my head stubbornly and got a slap from Gunther for my pains. After that he proceeded awkwardly to beat me, over Gail's protests. "You promised!" she cried.

Dr. Naldi took her by the arm and pulled her back a ways, and Gunther went to work in earnest. He had the right instincts, but he'd had no training. Besides, he was afraid of damaging his hands. It wasn't so bad. Wegmann stood back all the while with his gun, covering the situation and watching tolerantly, like an adult observing children at play. Presently he made an impatient sound and stepped forward.

"We're wasting time," he said. "Let him get dressed. We can continue this elsewhere if we must. Dr. Naldi, you've done a lot of driving in this country with all kinds of vehicles. Can we get his half-ton truck up the mountain? I don't want to leave it here."

Naldi looked at the empty capsule bitterly and flung it aside. "I would say yes, particularly if there's a set of tire chains to fit... What about it, Mrs. Hendricks?"

Gail said, "There are chains, you-all ought to know that."

Naldi frowned. "Why should we know that?"

"Well, after all, Wegmann took them off for us, down in Carrizozo, and besides, we had them on when one of your men tried to run us off the road in San Agustin Pass; that's why he failed."

"I have no knowledge of any such attempt," Naldi said. "Wegmann?"

The man with the gun shook his head. "I haven't been over that pass in months, nor sent anybody."

"Gunther?"

"Not me. I've been laying low since that trouble in Juarez; I've had no contact with anybody. Hell, I just crossed the border a few hours ago, and almost got caught in a dragnet at that!"

Naldi said, "Describe the incident, Mrs. Hendricks."

"Well, a man in a big gray car followed us from El Paso and... what's the matter?"

Wegmann had laughed. "A big gray car? An Oldsmobile, perhaps?"

"Why, yes. An Oldsmobile with Texas license plates." Wegmann was grinning. "It's all right," he said. "I know about that car. As a matter of fact, I buried it myself." He stopped grinning and became businesslike. "Gunther, you drive our four-wheel-drive job and lead the way. Keep an eye on the mirror in case we need help. Dr. Naldi, you can handle the pickup better than a gun, I think. You drive the truck and I'll ride in back with the prisoners... What is it now, Mrs. Hendricks?"

I felt kind of sorry for her, standing there looking startled and indignant. For a sophisticated woman, she was very naïve in some ways. She'd really expected they wouldn't hurt me, I guess. She'd even expected that they would let her go.

22

It was cold, lying in the back of the truck, face down, tied hand and foot. The fact that the piled-up duffel bags, suitcases, and supplies at the side of the narrow space barely left room for the two of us on the mattress didn't add to our comfort, although it did keep us from rolling around too much as the truck bounced and swayed.

Behind us, at the corner where the tailgate joined the side, Wegmann had made a blanket-padded nest for himself. He sat there, a dim shape in the darkness. My revolver, which he'd taken from Gail, rested on his knee. This made sense, professionally speaking. It was a nice, powerful little gun; and if you have to shoot a guy, it leaves less evidence if you can manage to do it with his own weapon.

I could feel Gail shivering beside me. She'd said nothing since we left the lodge. When you came right down to it, there wasn't a lot she could say—she'd pulled a double cross and it had backfired. The laugh, if any, was on her. For some reason I didn't feel very much like laughing. I managed to get a grip on the sleeping bag lying nearby, but when I tried to work it over us, for warmth, Wegmann reached forward and jerked it away.

"None of that," he said. "No covers. I want to see every knot clearly, Mr. Helm."

"Hell," I said, "you can't see anything in here, man." This wasn't strictly true. The windows of the canopy, coated as they were with frost, were beginning to show a faint gray dawn as we jolted up the unknown road to an unknown destination—unknown, at least, to me. Dr. Naldi, I noted, was an artist with the gears. It seemed like a strange skill for a learned Ph.D. to have picked up. A chain link had broken and was clanking rhythmically against the right rear fender. Well, those chains had seen me through several winters already.

"I can see enough," Wegmann said. "I can see if you move."

I was glad to have him talking at last. There were a couple of theories about him I wanted to check.

I said, "You're a pro, aren't you? Your name isn't Wegmann. I've seen your face in the files somewhere. The name was something Slavic." That was a guess, from the shape of his features. I hadn't seen his face in any file, or I'd have recognized him, but it would be useful to know if it was there to be found. He didn't speak; he wasn't giving anything away. I went on: "That dumb, flat-faced, country-boy look must come in handy in your line of work. But what are you doing here with a bunch of dressed-up amateurs and save-the-world-from-destruction crackpots?"

He hesitated; then I guess he decided it wouldn't hurt to relax and be himself for a little. Any cover is a strain to keep up, no matter how long you've been at it.

"Somebody must mind the store," he said, "while the children play their happy, destructive little games. Come to that, what are you doing here, Mr. Helm? If what the lady says is true, why would anybody send a good man after a flunky like Gunther? I know you're a pretty good man. That's why I let him have a little fun with you back there, I wanted the chance to size you up."

"Thanks," I said, "for the compliment, if nothing else. As for the question, do you get to ask why in your outfit? That's not the way I heard it."

"It is a point," he said. "But it is not an answer."

"Maybe they don't know he's a flunky," I said, choosing my words carefully. "Maybe they think he's the big wheel, the head man for this area, the fellow known as Cowboy. I told my chief he didn't have the weight for it. My chief said it wasn't our job to put him on the scales. Heavy or light, the word from Washington was Gunther."

"That is very interesting," Wegmann said. "That's very reassuring. That's what I hoped you would say, Mr. Helm. So they think he is this Cowboy they have hunted so long? Well, I worked hard enough to create that impression. I selected Mr. Gunther and trained him carefully, just for this purpose—of course, I did get some useful work out of him down in Juarez, but just between us, he doesn't make a very efficient operative. He has a tendency to lose his head. I allowed him to attract official attention gradually. Fortunately, he is a very stupid and conceited man who can't conceive of anybody being more clever than he is. Also, he is very hungry for money. And of course he does wear very conspicuous clothes."

"And Naldi?"

"Oh, Dr. Naldi is what you would call the inside man, the mad professor, you might say, who betrayed his country because of a wild theory. And stupid Hank Wegmann, the conscientious man at the filling station, was merely a convenient dupe for these smart people. He will escape, of course, but nobody will be very concerned about that, because he is not really important… You know, of course, why I am speaking to you frankly."

I laughed shortly. "I think I've been in the business as long as you, Wegmann. I know, all right."

"It is the only way," he said. "You understand. There is nothing personal."

"Sure," I said. "I'd do it myself, if the orders were to break clean and leave no witnesses."

"I am glad you understand."

Beside me, Gail stirred slightly, listening to this. A little intake of breath said she was about to speak, to ask a question, then she sighed and was still again. The truck jolted to an abrupt halt and somebody flung open the rear. Next there was the business of untying our feet and getting us unloaded, but I didn't pay too much attention to the details. Even if there was a break, I wasn't ready to take advantage of it yet. Besides, I was looking at the contraption they had installed in the church steeple.

Maybe it was a funny place to find a church, high on the side of the mountain, but that country is full of deserted mining camps and old ghost towns, and while many of the early settlers were pretty rough hombres, many were religious folk, too. Often the church was the best-built structure in the community—the last to fall down after the population moved elsewhere.

I'd guessed we were up on the Sierra Blanca somewhere, but we weren't quite as high as I'd thought. It had seemed, riding in back all trussed up, that we'd done enough climbing to be well above timber line, but there were still heavy stands of pine around us. The little forgotten town was wedged into a fold in the mountainside which opened to the west. There were some board shacks still standing, weathered silvery gray. A couple of stone huts remained almost intact, sturdily built of irregular pieces of local rock laid up carefully, Indian fashion, with mud mortar or no mortar at all. Roofless shells and stumps of walls, half buried in the snow, showed where other houses had been. Up the hillside, above the pines, was at least one mine shaft; there were probably others.

The squat little church was of stone, and parts of it had fallen into rubble, but sections of the roof remained, and most of the bell tower. Up there, camouflaged from air observation by the remnants of the wooden belfry, was the gadget. Actually, it was a kind of parabolic antenna which I associated with radar. You see similar rigs around most military installations, turning nervously, listening like great headless ears.

To be perfectly honest, I can't guarantee such rigs are concerned with radar; that's just what somebody told me once. Electronics isn't my field at all, any more than atomics. I won't even guarantee that this dingus was parabolical. It could have been hyperbolical or spherical, but it's my impression that the electronics boys have more fun with parabolas, for mathematical reasons we won't go into here.

Anyway, it was a bowl-shaped contrivance of rods and wires several feet in diameter. It was aimed in a general westerly direction—out towards the great open valley below—and it was searching busily, swiveling back and forth and up and down in an intricate pattern. There was a man up in the belfry with it. I didn't envy him his job. For one thing, it must have been cold, just sitting there, and for another, that old stonework hadn't been designed to support a lot of heavy, vibrating machinery.

Wegmann was standing beside me. "Well, Mr. Helm?" he said. "What do you think?"

I asked, "What does it do, catch flies and small birds?"

"Not small birds, Mr. Helm," he said. "Not small birds—large ones."

23

High in the old church, a hundred and fifty yards across the little gulch from where we had stopped at the edge of the pines, the radar-like gizmo continued to trace out its complex search pattern, looking more alive and intelligent and energetic than the few half-frozen people in the place. From one of the old stone huts came the incongruous putt-putt noises of an internal combustion engine, probably a diesel or gasoline generator. I stamped my feet to bring back circulation, wishing I could perform a similar favor for my hands, which were still tied behind me.

"What does he mean?" Gail asked, speaking for the first time since we'd left Ruidoso. "What is it? What is that thing, Matt?"

"You heard him. It's the Wegmann Electronic BirdCatcher, Mark I."

Wegmann shook his head, unsmiling. "You are mistaken, Mr. Helm; I am no scientist. The original device was invented, I believe, by a gentleman named

Hallenbeck, Dr. Rudolf Hallenbeck, a German physicist who was concerned with missile development for Hitler and sought refuge in the Soviet Union after World War II."

"Sought refuge," I said. "That's a nice way of putting it."

He shrugged "You got von Braun. We got Hallenbeck... Far from being Mark I, this is, I believe, the eleventh model produced, but only the fourth we have received here. Considering the difficulties of smuggling the machinery into the country and assembling it in a suitably desolate location, it can be understood that only the most promising versions reach us. The others failed to pass the preliminary tests on the Siberian missile ranges and were therefore not issued to us for field trials."

"I see," I said. "Field trials."

"An interesting concept, don't you think? What better way to test your equipment against the probable enemy's? We have been very careful. Down there, they still believe their chronic troubles to be due to stray radio transmissions of an innocent nature. They will know otherwise, of course, when they find what is left of the machine. We will not have time to dismantle and remove it, so we will have to destroy it. But we will not be here when they come."

Dr. Naldi, standing nearby, was regarding Wegmann with a puzzled air. "I don't understand," he said. "You speak of chronic troubles. I thought—"

"You thought this was the first machine of its kind, brought here with great difficulty and expense just to serve your purpose?" Wegmann laughed. "Well, perhaps we did give you some such impression, doctor. After all, you were looking for a miracle, were you not? You had appealed in vain to your government and the stubborn Dr. Rennenkamp to stop this dangerous test. You were willing to go to any extremes and accept help from anybody, in the name of humanity. Well, we supplied the help. Why should we make it look easy?"

"I see," Naldi said slowly. "I see."

"The only real miracle," said Wegmann, "is that we have come this close to success with no more assistance than we've got from you. You and Gunther botched your share of the operation miserably; not only that, but yesterday when you were about to be arrested, you came running to me for help instead of staying as far away from me as possible. You drew attention my way. So did Gunther, when he ran into trouble this side of the border. It is a real miracle that, between you, everything wasn't ruined. I suppose one can't expect absolute efficiency from non-professional personnel, but I did expect the two of you to make at least some attempt to follow the simple instructions you were given."

It was a real reaming-out, such as Naldi himself might have given a careless technician in his employ, and the scientist's face turned darkly red. His eyes grew narrow and angry behind his glasses.

"Really, Mr. Wegmann, what gives you the right to…?" Naldi checked himself, and sighed. "Well, perhaps there is some justice in what you say. This kind of melodrama is not in my line. Only desperate necessity forces me to assist in it. For the sake of mankind, Mr. Wegmann, that test must be stopped—or at least delayed until—"

"It will be stopped," Wegmann said.

"As for the films, I do not think it is fair to accuse me of complete failure. They must be here, somewhere."

"What makes you think so?"

Naldi frowned. "What do you mean?"

"What makes you think they must be here?" Wegmann glanced at me and laughed shortly. "My guess is that those precious films have been in Washington for days, if they were not destroyed in El Paso. It is a good thing that we did not count on being able to get our bearings from your copy of the government map, Dr. Naldi, but took the precaution of making a few sights while the weather was clear. We'd be in a serious predicament if we had to aim the apparatus visually this morning, with all this haze!"

He waved his arm to the west, where the morning haze still concealed the mountains on the far side of the great geological basin. Naldi did not look that way, however, nor did Gail. They were both staring at me in a startled way. Gail spoke first.

"You mean… you mean he never had them? But he told me—"

"I have no doubt he told you many things, Mrs. Hendricks," Wegmann said, "which you, to repay the grudge you bore him, promptly related to us, as he expected you to do."

"But—"

Wegmann gestured towards the hut from which came the sound of machinery. "Please. Your feet should be able to carry you now… Yes, what is it, Naldi?"

The scientist's face showed indignation. "Why didn't you tell us this earlier? Why did you let us… If he had no films, what was the point in setting such an elaborate trap? You deliberately let us make fools of ourselves capturing and searching—"

Wegmann said gently, "Dr. Naldi, you have never needed my permission to make a fool of yourself. The search was unnecessary of course. If you'll remember, I kept saying it was a waste of time. The capture, however, was absolutely necessary."

"But why, if there were no films?"

"Quite simply," Wegmann said, "because these two people had managed to obtain too much information about me to be left alive to talk, afterwards."

"You're going to kill them?" Naldi sounded shocked. Wegmann laughed and gestured towards the apparatus in the tower. "My dear doctor, how many people are you helping me kill with that? You're being naïve!"

"But that's different. That's… unfortunately, it is an essential step towards saving thousands of other lives, maybe millions. This is just cold-blooded murder!"

"Now you are simply playing with words," Wegmann said impatiently. "And I have a question for you, doctor. It has been reported to me that yesterday you tried to get Dr. Rennenkamp to further delay the test. Would you mind explaining why?"

"Well, I—"

"I had you arrange for one delay. It was necessary in order to get them out there precisely today. But another delay would have been fatal to our plans. You know that. Why did you try to talk Dr. Rennenkamp into another postponement?"

Naldi licked his lips nervously. Then, abruptly, he drew himself up and squared his shoulders. He spoke firmly, "Because I thought in another week it might be safe for them to make the shot. At least the risk would be much smaller; my instruments show that conditions are rapidly becoming much less critical. I thought, if I could get the old fool to hold off another week, just a few more days, we wouldn't have to go through with this terrible—"

"Naldi," said Wegmann, "you are a sentimental fool." He must have made some kind of a signal, although I didn't catch it. There was a sharp, explosive noise from the church tower, almost coincident with the crack of a rifle bullet going past and the unforgettable sound as it struck home. Naldi pitched back into the snow, dead before he fell.

"All right, Mrs. Hendricks," Wegmann said calmly. "That way, if you please. Follow the tracks carefully. We do not wish to disturb the snow unnecessarily."

Gail stared at him in a stunned way. Her eyes were very wide and her face was very white; the little freckles on her nose showed plainly. She turned her shocked stare towards the body at her feet. Dr. Naldi's bifocal lenses looked blindly up at the morning sky, askew in the dead, dark face. There was only a small spot of blood on the front of his coat. Gail made a choked sound and turning, stumbled away.

Wegmann gestured to me to follow. I obeyed, aware that Gunther and two men were covering the jeep station wagon he had driven here which had a ski rack on top for camouflage and my truck with white canvas that would presumably make them look like snow-covered boulders from the air. Maybe they had an extra sheet for the body. The other two men seemed unaffected, but Gunther looked a little sick.

Three men here, I thought, one in the tower with a rifle and Wegmann himself—five so far. Well, I'd offered myself as bait according to instructions. I really couldn't complain because too many had taken up the offer.

Ahead of me, Gail slipped to one knee, then picked herself up again awkwardly. Her bound wrists looked unreal and theatrical. The thing up in the tower looked phony, too, like something in a science-fiction movie. I paused under the church tower and looked up. From this angle, I couldn't see the rifleman, but the gadget itself was clearly visible.

"Nervous little beast, isn't it?" I said, with a backward glance at Wegmann, who was following at a discreet distance.

"It is only seeking now," he replied. "When it finds what it is seeking, it will lock on and commence tracking. It will report distance, direction and speed of flight to the instruments inside the church. When a certain switch is thrown, it will also assume control. We will be able to steer the big bird towards us, or to send it away—say to a suitable target far across the valley."

"When it takes off like that," I said, "assuming that it does, won't the range officer hit his little red button and blow it up?"

"The range safety officer will undoubtedly close the destruct circuit, or try to," Wegmann said. "He will be very much surprised, no doubt, when nothing happens. He will be even more surprised to discover that his test missile is armed. I have taken a long time to build my organization here, Mr. Helm, and it is a very good one. I have planned this demonstration well. Dr. Naldi merely helped me to select a suitable target. Your newspapers will have a great deal to write about in the next few days."

"When does the show start?" I asked.

"The bird flies at ten," he said, and gestured with the gun he still held—my gun. I found myself wishing that I'd thought to sabotage it in some way before passing it to Gail, but that would have been a dead give-away if discovered. "Please keep moving," Wegmann said. "Mrs. Hendricks is getting ahead of us. Don't try any clever delays or diversions, I warn you. I have a use for prisoners. There is someone I wish to keep occupied and unsuspicious for the next hour or so—you have that long if you are careful. But the exact number of prisoners does not really matter. I hope you understand."

"I read you," I said, "loud and clear."

Wegmann raised his voice. "Mrs. Hendricks. That's far enough. Wait for us there."

She stopped and waited at the door of the hut. I could feel the vibration of the machinery inside as I came up. Gail glanced at me briefly and looked away. A little color had returned to her face. She brushed snow off the knee of her pants. Wegmann reached us, waved us back with the gun, and opened the door. The noise of a big gasoline engine, along with the crackling hum of the generator it was driving and a breath of warm air smelling of hot oil and grease, came to us strongly.

"You will be comfortable in here, I hope," Wegmann said hospitably. Then he leaned forward and shouted to somebody inside. "Company, Mr. Romero!"

There was no answer, but he signaled us forward anyway. I followed Gail inside. The windows were blacked out; the only illumination came from a forty-watt bulb on a cord attached to one of the round log rafters— *vigas* they are called in that country. The machinery took up half the space in the little building. Inside the place, it made a fearful racket. I looked around for the man to whom Wegmann had yelled, assuming he'd be an engineer or mechanic on watch.

For a moment, I saw no one. Then Wegmann stepped past us and kicked at something in the corner.

"Don't play possum with me, Mr. Romero!" Wegmann shouted. "Here are some friends to keep you company. They'd like to ask you about an incident involving a gray Oldsmobile, haha!"

The bundle of clothing stirred and revealed itself to be a rather small man in a gabardine topcoat that was liberally smeared with the dirt and grease of the floor. His black hair, rather long, hung lankly into his face which—under the dirt—was quite pale except for some spectacular bruises. He had a small, black moustache. I was looking at the man who'd tried to run us off the road up in San Agustin Pass. I was looking at the M.C. of the Club Chihuahua.

24

I didn't let myself try to figure it out. One thing you learn early in the business is not to waste cerebral energy trying to solve the problems for which answers are already available at the back of the book. Our cellmate, whoever he might be, would undoubtedly tell us his sad story in due time—if we lived that long.

In the meantime, flat on my face on the dirt floor, I was busy using all the old muscle-tensing tricks to get a little slack for my ankles, which Wegmann was busy tying up. He gave me nothing that could really be called an opening—which was just as well. It wasn't him I wanted, but things were running pretty close now, and if I had seen a chance I'd have been very tempted to take it. There might be better ones later, but then again there might not.

"All right, Mrs. Hendricks," he shouted over the noise.

Gail hesitated and dropped awkwardly to her knees.

Wegmann gave her a shove that dumped her on her face, yanked her legs out straight and lashed them up.

"So," he shouted. "Now, I will leave you... Oh, make no elaborate, self-sacrificing plans about sabotaging that generator as the hour approaches, Mr. Helm. There are fully charged storage batteries in reserve, adequate to operate our equipment over the critical period. Stopping this machinery will merely deprive you of light and heat in here."

He stood up and looked us over, went over and rechecked the bonds of the character named Romero and left us alone with the noise and stink. Well, at least we weren't freezing.

"Gail," I called when the door had remained closed a reasonable period of time.

She turned her head to look at me. There was dust on her cheek and a kind of hopelessness in her eyes. She said something, but I couldn't make it out. I rolled over once, which brought our faces close together.

"He had him killed!" she gasped. "Naldi. One minute Naldi was standing there and then... and then he was *dead*! Like that!"

"Sure," I said. "Just like that. Now, listen..."

"You lied!" she cried. "From the start, you lied to me, tricked me, made love to me, used me..."

"Sure," I said. "And you lied to me, tricked me, made love to me and double-crossed me."

She stared at me for a long moment. Then she made a small, short, bitter sound that might have been a laugh. It was hard to tell with the noise.

She said more calmly, "He's going to kill us, too, isn't

he? If we don't... What can we do?"

It occurred to me she'd come a long way from the pampered Texas beauty who'd frozen in panic in San Agustin Pass. Like most people, it had turned out, she had a lot of hidden talents, some good, some bad.

"Listen closely," I said. "Something Wegmann said makes me think we'll have company in here pretty soon, and I think I know who it'll be. When he comes, you blow your top. Flip it good, understand? You can't stand being tied up, you're revolted by this filthy floor, you're going crazy with the terrible noise, get it? Make a goddamn spectacle of yourself. Create a diversion. Okay?"

She hesitated. "Do you think... do you think it will work?"

"What will work? Don't worry about anything like that; that's my department. Try to be a real actress, glamor girl. You're a woman in terror for her life. Don't think about your lousy pride, or your appearance, and don't, for God's sake, give one thought or look to me or what I may be doing. That'll wreck it instantly."

She was silent again. Her eyes studied my face for several seconds. Her tongue came out to moisten her lips.

"All right," she breathed. "All right, Matt."

I said, "And now let's get over and confer with the mysterious gent behind you. If you roll over twice, you'll be just about there."

"All right," she said again, but she didn't move at once. "Darling," she said.

"Yes?"

"You bastard," she said. "You lousy, calculating bastard."

I grinned at her. "You bitch," I said. "You dirty, double-crossing bitch."

She gave me a funny, shaky little smile, lying there, very close to me. Then she hunched herself around a bit, preparing for the awkward journey back into the corner. I saw her start and turn her head quickly. The man called Romero reared up just beyond her, having apparently made the trip while we were talking. His lips moved. I shook my head to indicate I couldn't hear a word.

It took us several minutes to get all three of us sitting up cozily, heads together, so we could converse above the engine noise.

"All right," I said to Romero, "let's start with you. You're a ham with a mike and a cheap tuxedo, telling the girls to take it off all the way. You're a lousy mountain driver. What else are you?"

"Listen—" he began angrily.

Then he checked himself, grinned and spoke one word. I stared at him. I don't mean that it proved anything conclusively. In a government the size of ours, you can't supply a universal, reliable recognition signal for all undercover agencies; there'd be a leak somewhere. Anyway, I guess we just don't trust each other enough to put our fives in each others' hands, which is what it would amount to under certain circumstances.

But there is a word of sorts, changed from time to time, and he had the current one. So, probably, did every foreign agent from Maine to California. As I say, it didn't prove a thing—except that it made a lot of things that had happened make sense at last. I gave him the proper countersign. His eyes widened slightly.

"Jim Romero," he said.

"Matt Helm," I said. We don't use the code names with outsiders, "Why the hell don't you watch where you're driving?"

"Why the hell don't you watch where you're kicking?" He grimaced. "My God, what a foul-up! Did you have any trouble with Peyton?"

"What about Peyton?"

"He's my boss on this job. I put him on your trail after I missed you in the mountains. He said, if he saw you, he'd have you watched until the time came, and then pick you up in the general roundup he was planning just before the test."

"He won't thank you for the tip," I said. "He met with a kind of accident. I kind of had to jump on him with both feet."

"So he went for you himself? I figured he'd want the credit of getting those films back." Romero made another face. "Tough, aren't you? You and your damn big feet! Where was Peyton's Man Friday while this was going on?"

"Bronkovic?" I said. "Why, he was trying to kill me, but the lady, here, got to work with a blunt instrument in the nick of time."

"Bronkovic isn't a bad guy," Romero said. "Peyton you can jump on all day, as far as I'm concerned. I suppose you have guys like that in your outfit."

"Maybe," I said, "but we try not to give them quite so much authority. Just where did you come into this, anyway? What were you doing down in Juarez?"

He said grimly, "I was doing all right, until you people butted into the case, that's what I was doing. I had a swell cover as M.C. in the joint, and everything was going fine. Then, first, along came that girl of yours who went over—I suppose she was yours. We may have our Peytons, but at least our female agents don't fall into bed with the first handsome creep with a fast line... Well, never mind that. She was kind of a nice kid, but mixed-up as hell in both the sex and politics departments: a real naïve save-the-world type, fundamentally." After a moment, he glanced at Grail. "Excuse me, ma'am. I forgot. She was your sister, wasn't she? I heard you say so that night, up on the stage there."

"It's all right," Gail said dryly. "We're all kind of mixed up in my family. If we weren't, I wouldn't be here."

"And then," Romero said to me, "just as we had things all set up to catch everybody with the goods— Naldi, your girl, Gunther, everybody—this lady comes wandering into the trap with Gunther. Well, that was all right. More grist for the mill, we figured. Then somebody heaved a knife and everything went to hell. None of my people could get where they were supposed to, the way everybody was milling around. You practically ruined me when I tried a fast retrieve—and who the hell were you? You ran off with the lady and the goods, saving the day for the other side, as it looked to us. Gunther got away in the confusion. Naldi... well, we had nothing conclusive on Naldi, so there wasn't anything we could do but keep an eye on him. He was too big to grab on mere suspicion. It was a mess."

"Tough," I said. "If your chief in Washington had been willing to cooperate with mine, we might all have got together in time."

"Hell, your girl went over," Romero said. "He wasn't going to explain our set-up to you after that, maybe putting us all in jeopardy—me, for instance, making love to that damn mike in broken English. Anyway, there wasn't a damn thing for me to do, afterwards, but take off after you and try to get the films back. I sent a query to Washington on you, of course, but I guess nobody was speaking to anybody by that time."

"What films?" I said. "They were sent off the next morning."

"How was I to know that. You *did* have them. At least she did," he said with a gesture towards Gail. "I was lying there on the stage, groaning loudly, remember, while they were being passed. *Wegmann, Carrizozo*, the kid said before she died. I heard that. It was a new name to us; I thought it might be a lead. I gave it to Peyton with the rest of it, of course; but he said for me to work on it myself and try to do a better job than I'd done to date. You know that damn, cold, sneering voice of his." Romero grimaced. "I guess I got over-eager, so here I am."

"How did they catch you?"

"I was watching the filling station. A character in a power wagon drove in and made contact with Wegmann. I followed when the guy left. He came up in this direction. I was doing fine, shadowing him just like the manual says. Then I got stuck in the snow. That damn snow!"

"That'll teach you to follow a four-wheel-drive truck with an ordinary sedan," I said, "and when will you border characters learn the use of chains?"

"When we get enough snow to practice on regularly," Romero said, "instead of just being buried in it once every couple of years. I was busy trying to dig out when they jumped me. They ditched the car somewhere and brought me here. It doesn't make me look very brave and bright, I know. Now let's hear about you."

I told him enough to bring him up to date—enough to make him look curiously at Gail, revising his first opinion of her in the light of the information I'd given him. I guess he'd assumed she was one of us, a pro or at least a loyal and dedicated amateur. She didn't like my telling him so much, but we were all going to have to work together, and it was no time to horse around with the truth out of regard for her sensitive feelings.

"Stop glaring at me and get your hands up front here, glamor girl," I said. "Pull my shirt out of my pants. Make me look real untidy. I don't have far to go, after the way they worked me over down there, I guess."

She gave me a surprised look. "Pull your... In heaven's name, why?"

"Don't ask," I said. "Just do... So there you have it,

Jaime," I said, pronouncing it Haymie, Spanish fashion.

"The name is Jim," he said stiffly.

"Jesus!" I said. "The bird flies at ten, and I have to consider your tender Castilian pride, Mr. Romero? Call me gringo if it makes you feel better." I glanced irritably at Gail. "Watch it, I'm ticklish there... Now help me work the belt buckle around to the back where I can get at it."

I hadn't thought about it up to that moment. I hadn't let a picture of it form in my mind. I hadn't let the words be part of my vocabulary. There had been no such thing as belt or buckle. After all, Wegmann had been around. If I could think of it, he could.

"Slip it around," I said. "The belt loops are big enough, unless somebody's miscalculated badly. If you hear anybody coming, flop the shirt down over it."

Romero said, "Ten o'clock is the time? It must be well past nine already."

I said, "Of course, something may abort the flight. It sometimes happens. Or the thing may blow up on the launching pad or whatever they fire it from. If so, it'll make quite a bang, from what Wegmann said."

"We wouldn't be so lucky," Romero said. "If they were sending up one of the new ones, maybe, but this is straight routine, I understand, just to give some instruments a ride and check a few tracking procedures."

"I'm surprised they'd shoot at all with all those important people on the reservation."

"There would have been no conflict if Rennenkamp's bunch hadn't postponed a week. Anyway, they're well over to the west, protected by half a range of mountains. I guess somebody figures it's safe to go ahead on schedule. Those old Wotans are reliable as streetcars nowadays."

"What's a Wotan?" Gail asked. "What happens at ten? What are you talking about, anyway?"

"Dear lady," Romero said, "a Wotan is a lousy damn guided missile of the ground-to-ground variety. That is, it's fired from the surface and hits a target on the surface instead of going off to chase airplanes or something. In other words, it's a kind of self-propelled artillery shell, a great big bullet with a brain. Not the giant intercontinental kind they fire at Canaveral, of course, but big enough. You don't want to be around where it lands. *Comprende*?"

"Well, vaguely, but—"

"This particular Wotan," the little dark-haired guy said, "will be armed and sabotaged in certain ways, Wegmann claims… Has he taken you on his guided tour, Matt?"

"No, I guess he thought there wasn't time."

"He showed me around when he first brought me up here. They're all alike, these masterminds. After working undercover so long, they like to share their triumphs with somebody. He's very proud of that thing in the tower."

"So I noticed," I said. "What bothers me is, if it's half as good as he seems to think, why does he want to tell the world all about it? I should think they'd keep it as their ace military secret."

"I wouldn't know," Romero said. "It hadn't occurred to me… He didn't say anything about that. He did say it was going to create a world-wide sensation and impress a lot of people with the power of Soviet science. There's no doubt he's right, if he can really pull it off."

"Can he?" I asked.

"Something's been raising hell with our missile tests down here, for years, off and on. There's never been a really good explanation for it. He claims to be it. If he is…"

Gail said angrily, "Look, I'm just a poor little Texas girl who flunked math and physics. Will you bright, bright men just tell me in words of one syllable what it's all about?"

I said, "Honey, at ten o'clock, if Wegmann's got the time right, that missile will take off and come whistling up the range. A bullet with a brain, Jim just said. A brain that can take orders. Well, our friend Wegmann has a machine that gives orders. You saw it. Now do you understand?"

"But—"

"At a certain number of seconds or minutes past ten," I went on, "that gizmo in the tower will pick up the approaching Wotan and assume control, blanking out all other signals in some way, don't ask me how. Then Wegmann will swing his sights around towards that camp across the valley, full of congressmen and senators and scientific geniuses including Dr. Rennenkamp himself. Even if Wegmann can't see it from here, he's already got the bearing, you heard him say so. I don't suppose his machine is bothered by a little haze. And the big bird, if everything works right, will just ride the beam right down into camp… Can they actually turn one of those things through ninety degrees?" I asked Romero.

He shrugged. "Wegmann says so, this type, anyway."
Gail said, "You mean… you mean just sitting here he's
going to blow up all those people? Why, that's downright
horrible!"

That, I thought, was quite an understatement, in her
soft Texas voice. I thought of Buddy McKenna, over in the
shadow of the Manzanitas. *Illegitimati non carborundum*,
he'd told me. Don't let the bastards grind you down. He'd
had a premonition, I guess, the kind good newsmen get…

I said, "Does it matter whether Wegmann is sitting or
standing when he does it?" Then I raised my voice and
cried, "What the hell do you think you're doing? Who
invited you to the conference? Don't you come sucking
around here, you treacherous slut!"

I gave her a shove with my shoulder that sent her
sprawling.

25

It was that damn racket. I should have been watching the door, of course, and I thought I was, but you get in the habit of depending on your ears as well as your eyes—and ears were no use in there. My vigilance must have slipped for a moment. Suddenly Gunther was there, pistol in hand—the little nickel-plated weapon with which he'd shot LeBaron, by the looks of it—closing the door behind him.

We were all acting much too cozy and friendly, sitting there like three monkeys on a stick. Something had to be done about it fast, and I did it. Maybe it was a little rough on Gail, but on the other hand, it gave her a good springboard from which to dive into her act. After the first moment of shock, I saw understanding come to her. She started to look around, but checked herself in time. Her face puckered up nicely, and a couple of real tears trickled down her cheeks, as she stared at me reproachfully.

Gunther was above us now. "I declare," he said, "a real pretty tableau. Let's see those ropes!"

He checked my bonds and Romero's, then went over to Gail, who was curled up in a woeful little ball, watering the floor with her tears. He tested the ropes on her wrists and ankles, and nudged her with his foot.

"Turn it off, honey," he shouted. "This is Sam, Precious. Remember Sam, the guy who knows you like a book?"

Anyway, he said something like that. It was hard to make out the exact words through the steady, pounding racket. I wanted to tell him he was dead, standing there in his big hat and high-heeled boots. That was what he'd been put here for, of course. He thought he was being given the responsible job of watching the prisoners, but Wegmann had given me the hint, and I knew Mr. Gunther was merely being kept on ice, so to speak, until Wegmann decided how best to dispose of him along with the rest of us. He'd been groomed for the part of Cowboy, and he was going to play it dead.

I started to shout at him, to tell him so, but he would have thought it a trick to turn him against his friends—an old, corny trick to try on a smart man like him. It was better to let Gail handle it. She'd stopped sobbing at the touch of his foot. Now she raised her head, turning her streaked face up to him.

"Oh, Sam!" she cried. "Sam, I'm so glad to see you, honey! You're going to help me, aren't you? We've always been friends, haven't we, Sam? You're not going to let them…" She stumbled prettily and convincingly over the words, "…kill me?"

"Why the hell should I help you, Precious?" he asked.

"Oh, Sam," she said, "you can't fool me, honey. I know you're good and kind…"

I lost the rest of that, as she lowered her voice slightly. She wasn't following the script I'd roughed out for her, which was all right, but I was afraid she was overdoing it a little. It was pretty crude. But she knew her man better than I did.

"Good and kind, am I, honey?" Still interested, he laughed at her, lying at his feet.

"Yes, they tried to tell me you killed Janie—had her killed—but I know you didn't do anything of the sort. I just know it!"

I didn't like that at all. I could see that she might want the final word on her sister's death, but it was the wrong place for detective work. I was getting the belt buckle around back where I wanted it, under cover of my disordered shirt, but if she annoyed him and lost his attention I'd have a hard time preparing and using it with him watching, particularly since my fingers seemed to have no feeling and hardly any strength.

I lost some more conversation with all the noise. He was laughing again. "…so you think you know Sam Gunther, all you rich bitches doling out a little money here and a little there in return for a lot of flattery and a bit of loving? Well, the time is coming, Precious, when you'll be doing the flattering and I'll be handing out the money… As for your sister, she was sent to kill me, did you know that. To kill me!" He sounded shocked. "She broke down and told me so herself!"

Gail said something I couldn't hear over the noise.

"That's right," he shouted back, "but I could always get around her, remember? I had her eating right out of my hand. She was still in love with me, and she had a guilty conscience a mile wide, after what she'd tried to do. Also, she was a sucker for Dr. Naldi's pitch, the silly little fool… Well, she wasn't so little, come to think of it. She was a well-stacked kid; she really looked good on that stage, I'll give her that. It was kind of a pity. But she knew too much, and things were getting tight. I didn't want her delivering the evidence to me with a couple of coppers watching. So I snapped my fingers, just like that." He snapped his fingers. "I can kill, too, Precious, if they force me to it. And when I'm through, I'll have more men around me like the man who threw the knife that night, tough men, dangerous men, just waiting for me to snap my fingers again!"

She said something else, and he said something else, still telling her what a big man he was going to be some day. Or words to that effect. His type are always going to be big men some day. I'd heard the routine before so many times I didn't bother to listen to the Gunther version. They're always small men wanting to be big, and they never make it. They always wind up stooges for pros like Wegmann.

But he was giving me time, and that was fine, but then he stopped talking and started to move away. That wasn't good. If he got to sitting down on the wooden stool over by the engine with his gun ready, watching, I'd never manage to do what needed to be done, unseen, with my clumsy, bound hands.

"Sam!" Gail pleaded desperately. "Please, Sam! I don't care about Janie; I'm sorry I mentioned it! She hated me anyway, and you know why! Sam, please, you've got to help me! You've got to! Why, I wouldn't be here if it wasn't for you!"

He stopped and frowned and came back. "Who're you trying to kid, Precious?" he shouted. "You came up here with this guy, because you were so mad at him. You told us all about it down in Carrizozo, remember? You were getting back at him because he'd treated you disrespectfully, or something, back in El Paso."

"Yes, that's what I told you," she admitted. "I was too proud to admit that I… Not to your face, Sam; not with people listening. Don't you understand? He was going to kill you. I had to do something to prevent it, to warn you, to help you… Don't you understand, Sam? I did it for you!"

I didn't think he'd buy it. It was pretty damn corny. He looked down at her for a moment in silence, thinking it over. I saw to my surprise that be was flattered and intrigued. He'd made his living off women for years. I guess it came as no real surprise that there was one more in the world who found him irresistible.

He started to speak, then changed his mind. He laughed shortly, and turned away. He went over to the engine with a backward glance and sat down on the stool with his elbows on his knees, both hands supporting the little nickel-plated pistol aimed at us.

"Sam!" Gail cried. "Sam, please! You've got to believe me!"

He laughed, over there, and pointed to his ear, indicating that he couldn't hear a word. She started to move, and he watched with great interest, clearly wondering if she'd really do it. I mean, it isn't every man who can get a beautiful woman to come crawling to his feet, proclaiming her love.

I tried not to watch it. I mean, there are only three ways you can transport yourself any distance when your hands and feet are bound. You can roll like a log, you can squirm along on your side like a snake, or you can sit up and kind of skid yourself along on the seat of your pants. None of these modes of locomotion is anything you really want to see being employed by an attractive woman for whom you have respect and affection…

But it held his attention, that was the main thing. I guess he'd had to take a certain amount of stuff from her in the past; she might play, but she had kept him in his place. Watching the rich, arrogant and lovely Mrs. Hendricks, bound hand and foot, making her way across the oil-stained floor at considerable expense to her dignity and clothing, was a real treat to him.

The gun barrel drooped, as his eyes remained fixed on the slender, struggling, disheveled figure slowly drawing closer. It was time for me to reach under my shirt in back and peel the metal foil from the sharp edges of the trick belt buckle Mac had given me and cut the ropes on my wrists.

I got hold of the buckle all right. I even found a purchase for my fingernails, but that was as far as it went. I didn't have the strength to take it from there.

26

You understand, the buckle was made of steel with the edges honed to razor sharpness, and in order to keep it from disemboweling me every time I bent over, it was clad in metal foil, carefully decorated with an Indian pattern, so that it looked like the massive, ornate silver buckles offered to tourists on both sides of the border.

In theory, it should have taken only an instant to strip off the foil and bring the edges into action, but the fellow who'd figured out the theory obviously hadn't taken into account the fact that the buckle might have to be used by a beat-up gent who'd had his hands tied tightly behind him—in cold weather—for several hours. Like so many of the nice stunts thought up in Washington, it just didn't work. The foil was too heavy.

I scratched at it feebly, but it might as well have been soldered on—and the distance Gail had left to travel was getting shorter by the minute. Gunther was getting tired of the entertainment, anyway. I saw him speak, although I couldn't hear the words; then he rose and went to her. He set her on her feet and made a show of brushing her off magnanimously. He helped her hop to the stool on which he'd been sitting—I'd forgotten to mention that way of traveling, bound. You can hop, if your balance is good or you have someone to steady you.

She was speaking, as she sat down. He listened to her for a moment. I don't know what line she was trying to feed him now, probably telling him how she'd yearned for him since childhood. I saw his face go angry. He lifted a hand and slapped her off the stool, looked down at her for a moment, frowning, glanced around suspiciously and came stalking over to check on Romero and me.

I couldn't get that damn heavy foil off, and it was too late to cut myself loose, anyway, but I did have the belt unbuckled, ready to slip out of the loops. I didn't know what Romero was doing and I didn't really care. He seemed to be a nice enough guy when he wasn't behind the wheel of a car, but he'd been here a day or so without accomplishing much, and I don't have much faith in those security people, anyway. There wasn't any sense in counting on him. I'd have to do it by myself, if I could.

As Gunther approached, holding the gun slackly, not really expecting trouble, I made a big demonstration of trying to rear up and meet him on my feet. He stopped and brought the pistol to bear, watching me warily. I lost my balance and did a comic back fall, landing heavily, hoping my boots weren't too big for the trick that came next, that is, if he gave me a chance to use it by looking away briefly.

I have long arms, as well as long legs, and in tennis or street shoes I can usually manage to get my feet between my bound wrists, bringing my hands in front of me. It's a handy stunt for a man in my line of work, and I'd practiced it from time to time, but never in winter clothes with boots on.

I waited, acting jarred by the fall. Gail had struggled up behind Gunther, but much too far away to reach him. She tried a couple of hops in his direction and fell painfully. He glanced around and laughed, and then I heard somebody shout over the pounding motor noises—and there was Romero on his feet, hopping like a kangaroo straight at Gunther.

Gunther turned. The gun came up, but Romero didn't stop. It was a brave thing, but it was no time for me to be watching the show on the screen; I had business to attend to. I was dragging my wrists over my boots, losing plenty of skin, as the gun went off; then I was on my feet, grabbing the belt and pulling it clear. I heard the bullet hit, and saw Romero kind of hunch up and fall, but I had my weapon ready. It's best used as a sort of murderous brass knucks, with the leather wrapped around the fist and the buckle out, but my hands were tied, and I needed more range than that to reach my man, anyway.

Like most novices at murder, he had to admire his handiwork briefly. He couldn't just shoot one guy and turn to deal with the next, he had to watch the first one fall. Maybe he wasn't quite sure of his marksmanship; maybe he enjoyed seeing him drop. I had plenty of time to get set, and I got him as he turned.

I raised both arms and swung the heavy buckle at the end of the strap. It sang through the air like one of those Japanese noisemakers you whirl on a string. It caught him just right, squarely across the face, and with that much power behind it, the foil made no difference at all. I couldn't have done better, or worse, with a machete.

He lost the gun and staggered backward, screaming, covering his face with his hands. I took another hop and cut again, laying his hands open. I stood over him as he went down, using the belt as a flail until he no longer moved or yelled. Unfortunately, he had only fainted. The buckle hadn't cut deeply. But there were a few things to be attended to before I finished the job; besides, I preferred to do it without witnesses—particularly official government witnesses like Romero. Mac had specified a smooth, discreet and competent job, remember?

I hopped over to the little man, lying doubled up on the floor.

"How bad, Dad?" I shouted over the steady noise of the big engine.

He raised his head with an effort. "Just a scratch," he said.

"Yeah," I shouted. "I know those little .32 caliber scratches. Hold this one for me."

I sat down beside him and gave him the buckle to hold. There was no more trouble with the foil. Gunther had already helped peel it back here and there; I got the rest of it off without any trouble. Then I cut myself loose, hands and feet, and did the same for Romero. I went over and got Gunther's pistol. One shot had been fired from it, but he had extra cartridges in his pocket.

When I got back, Romero was sitting up. His face was even pastier-looking, under the dirt, than it had been.

"What's the time?" he yelled. "My watch stopped yesterday."

"Ten minutes of ten," I said, "according to this one, but I don't guarantee it."

"That gives us," he said, "just ten minutes to get over there and stop them."

"Us?" I said. "I came for this jerk and I've got him right here. I've lost nothing in any churches."

He looked startled; then he looked outraged and angry. "You crummy bastard," he shouted, "doesn't it matter to you that people are going to get killed, people this country can't afford to lose?"

I grinned at him. "The way Naldi talked, there'll be more damage than that if they're allowed to go through with the damn test. Wegmann's doing us all a big favor." I let him stew a moment longer; then I held out the little gun. "Can you shoot one of these things? First, can you walk?"

"Don't worry about me," he said, getting to his feet. "Amigo," I said, "about people who try to run me off mountain roads, my worry-quotient is infinitesimal. Five minutes from now you can fall down dead and I'll never miss you. But in the meantime, can you knock that marksman out of the tower before he gets more than one running shot at me?"

He looked at me for a moment. Then he grimaced. "I thought you said... Ah, hell. I'll do the running. You shoot."

"You can hardly stand up," I pointed out. "Besides, a runt like you'd bog down in the snow. I've got more road clearance. Let's hope he's a lousy shot at moving targets. I'll head so he has to expose himself to take a bead. Get him when he makes his try. Okay?"

He took the nickel-plated pistol. "With this? Well, if it won't shoot that far, maybe I can throw it. What's the time now?"

I took my watch off and gave it to him. "You're so nervous about the time, you keep track of it. Give me a minute, first, while I tie up my specimen."

"Make it thirty seconds," he said.

I used the odds and ends of rope to do a reasonable job on Gunther, who still didn't stem very interested in the proceedings. *Espionage and sabotage are not our concern,* Mac had said. I had no business at all haring off to make a target of myself, leaving my job unfinished. It was an inexcusable neglect of duty, a regrettable display of sloppy humanitarianism, or something, and I felt pretty good as I finished tying the knots and got to my feet. A man's got to flip it every now and then.

"Want a Band-Aid or something before we go?" I asked Romero.

He shook his head. He seemed to be waiting for me to attend to something else. When I frowned at him questioningly, he gestured towards Gail.

I said, "Don't be silly. I told you about her. Come on."

He looked startled. I saw Gail's eyes go wide. She may not have caught the words from where she lay, still tightly bound, but she got the meaning all right. I was surprised at both of them. What I was doing with Romero was a breach of orders and a display of poor judgment; I certainly wasn't going to compound it by turning loose a female who'd already betrayed me once—a woman who, even if her loyalties were in the right place now, had no training, no experience, and could only get in the way.

I mean, even looking at it from her point of view, she was safer right there, tied up to keep her out of trouble and mischief. The fact that she'd given us a hand just now didn't buy her any voting stock in the corporation.

I turned my back on her and went to the door. It all went like clockwork from there. I went leaping through the snow like a gazelle; the rifleman leaned out and got his shot but missed, and Romero, using the doorjamb of the hut for a rest, got a two-handed grip on the little revolver and picked him off like a pipe in a shooting gallery. The sniper swayed against the railing up there. The rifle slipped out of his hands and came down butt first into the snow at the base of the tower.

This was a little bonus I hadn't expected. I dropped the belt I was carrying for want of a better weapon, grabbed up the rifle, worked the bolt and was ready when the church door opened. Romero was ready, too. The man in the doorway, hit twice, never even twitched as he fell.

I went in over his body. A second man fired and made a

run for the tower stairway. I fired from the hip and missed; I never can get used to a rifle in close-range work. Romero, coming in behind me, shot at the disappearing legs and— from the sound of the yelp—nicked one of them. The little man could shoot. I looked at the bank of instruments along the wall and raised the rifle butt. Romero caught my arm.

"No," he said. There was a thoughtful look on his face. "Not that way."

Somebody up in the tower took a shot downward through the rotten roof. The bullet hit the dirt floor behind us. We moved closer to the instrument board. More shots were fired, all misses. I guess they were afraid of scrambling their own circuits with a misplaced bullet. "Make up your mind, amigo," I said.

Romero's face was greenish white. I'd never seen a live man look so ready for burial. I remembered that I owed him an apology for some derogatory thoughts I'd had about security men. A few little guys like this made up for a lot of Peytons. He slipped his hand under his waistband, feeling around in an absent way and brought it out with blood on it. Well, I'd already guessed that. When deer, elk or man hunches up like that when shot, it's always in the guts.

"You've got your job," he said. "I've got mine, to protect..." He stopped, as pain hit him. I guess the numbness was wearing off. "To apprehend..."

"Sure," I said. "Well, if we smash this thing, we protect. We can apprehend later."

He shook his head. "Wegmann talked about it," he

said, looking at the rows of knobs and switches. "He told me… he told me… He was proud of it. I told you that."

"Yes," I said. Somebody took another shot through the roof and missed again. "You told me."

"He showed me around… I don't know just what we'd have to cut or smash to make absolutely sure… A lot of it's only for monitoring. There's only one thing… one thing…" He drew a cautious breath. "Hell, I'm wandering. Get out of here, fast. You've got about five minutes."

"Wegmann?"

Gunther might be my job, but still I didn't feel right about leaving Wegmann.

"Give me the rifle," Romero said. "I can hold him in the tower long enough, until…" He grimaced with pain. "He'll be taken care of. I give you my word. They'll all be taken care of. I know just how to do it. Just run like hell and leave it to me."

I said, "It sounds like an attractive proposition, Señor Romero."

"Mister," he said.

"Sure," I said. "Mister."

"Get clear," he said. "As far as you can. See you in hell or somewhere."

I ran. I mean it was his job, and he talked as if he knew what he was about. I had my own work to do. Somebody took a couple of shots at me from the tower, but it takes a damn good pistol shot to hit a running target at any range. I hurled myself through the door of the generator hut and brought up short.

Gail was still on the floor, approximately where I'd left her, still bound. By her hands lay a small penknife, open. Beside the penknife lay some pieces of rope, but that was all. There was no sign of Gunther. I went quickly to the door, but of course he was nowhere to be seen. There were, however, some marks in the snow. I studied these for a moment and saw where they led. I grinned slowly.

I went back to Gail and cut her loose. She sat up and started to rub her wrists, not looking at me. I pulled her to her feet. For a tall and lovely lady, she looked remarkably like a truant kid, standing there defiantly, her face filthy with dust and tears, her sweater grimy and awry, her silly sexy pants smeared with dirt and grease from the engine-room floor.

"So you helped cut him loose," I said. "And he left you here to rot, just like I did. Smart man. He knows you, too."

"Matt, I—"

"Never mind," I said. "Now we run. Make for the truck and pay no attention to those jerks in the tower. They'll just be shooting at us with pistols, very inferior weapons. Think nothing of it. We've only got a couple of minutes, so we'll do our praying later. Okay?"

They did their best with what they had, but it wasn't enough. I saw Gail falter once as a bullet tugged at her sleeve; I had a bad moment when she fell headlong, but that was just a slip in the snow. She was up again and running instantly. I got a hole in one pants leg. Then we were out of pistol range. Laboring towards the truck at a slower rate, we saw bloodstains in the snow ahead of us. There were also stains on the white camouflage canvas covering the truck.

Well, where else could Gunther hide, when you came to think of it? Cut up as he was, he wouldn't want any part of the ruckus in the tower. In the truck was stuff that could be torn up for bandages, a means of escape if he had the strength, bedding to keep him warm if he didn't… I heard a low, shuddering moan from inside the truck. I looked in. Even in the semi-darkness, it wasn't hard to tell that Gunther was more dead than alive.

"Matt, look!"

I turned impatiently. Gail was pointing. The shooting had stopped. Up in the tower, the bowl-shaped antenna had ceased tracing its tricky scanning pattern. For a moment, I thought Romero, below in the church, had managed to cut off the power; then I saw the thing was still moving, but very slowly, tracking something high and distant and invisible coming up fast from the south. It sounds silly to say so, but the gadget had that intent, vibrant, triumphant look that a good quail dog gets when he has the covey located without a shadow of doubt.

Well, it was Romero's problem, and he'd indicated he knew how to deal with it. He'd said get clear. Left and out, LeBaron had said. If I didn't watch myself, I was going to get in the habit of leaving pretty good men behind in awkward situations.

"Come on," I said. "Let's put it on the road, such as it is."

I yanked the white canvas off. They'd left us the keys, which was nice of them. I had to make a swing towards the church, since they'd parked the truck facing that way, but nobody shot at us. They seemed to be very busy up there. Then we were heading up the slope away from the place.

"Matt," Gail said, "you've got to understand—"

"I know," I said. "You told me before. You're a proud woman."

"When you left me like that, after the way I'd humiliated myself trying to help you—"

There was a pause while the engine roared and the gears screamed and the tire chains fought for traction on the snowy slope. We came over the shoulder of the hill and dropped behind it, following the mountainside to the left. The road was just a snow-covered ledge with a deep ravine to the right. Scattered pines thrust upwards from the steep drop.

Gail laughed softly. Her hand touched my arm. "Anyway, you came back," she said.

I saw the thing coming. I've been told you don't usually see them; that when they're passing at full thrust they go too fast for the human eye to pick up at close range, but there's also something called peripheral vision… Anyway, I saw it out of the corner of my eye, sharp and clear for an instant, a wicked, wedge-shaped thing striking out of the sky.

"Hit the basement," I said.

I grabbed her in my arms and dove for the floor, letting

the truck take care of itself. I had a moment of regret for the sturdy old vehicle, as it wavered, untended on the steep road; then the shockwave picked it up as if it were a toy and tossed it into a ravine.

27

With the usual Washington logic, the underground test in the Manzanitas was postponed. The threat of sabotage was past, the desert roads were passable again, so they put it off another week over Rennenkamp's screams and howls of protest.

Experts were called in, and they could detect no harmonic vibrations in the earth's crust. They stated firmly that the North American continent was no more subject to massive instability, whatever that might be, than any other, and that no continent was in the slightest danger of suffering collapse under the stimulus of such a relative fleabite—compared to real geologic forces— as the explosion of a nuclear weapon anywhere, above-ground or below. The kindest view was that Naldi had simply flipped, poor fellow. There were also less charitable attitudes in evidence.

Well, all that was none of my business. I spent the week in and around Alamogordo, getting bawled out by people in and out of uniform. They admitted that it might be unreasonable to expect me to produce a complete circuit diagram of a mass of electronic equipment I'd only seen the outside of for about a minute, under fire, but they couldn't understand why the hell I couldn't at least produce an accurate sketch of the antenna.

Somebody turned up a report on Peyton and Bronkovic, two loyal and experienced security men who had been brutally assaulted in a motel room registered in my name. This odd circumstance got quite a play until the official word on the matter came through and the whole subject was dropped into the pool of embarrassed silence reserved for inter-departmental boo-boos.

The final verdict in my case was that I was probably a well-meaning cluck, but that a man who could retain so little useful information was one hell of an intelligence officer to be working for Uncle Sam. I didn't bother to point out that I wasn't an intelligence officer and that my training hadn't been along the lines of retaining information...

They let up on me gradually, but warned me to hang around in case they thought of anything else to ask, so I was stuck in Alamogordo. I was drinking alone in the motel bar when a young lieutenant came up. His face looked vaguely familiar; he'd been hanging around in a minor capacity through the interrogations.

"I guess we gave you a pretty rough time, sir," he said. "May I buy you a drink by way of apology?"

"Sure," I said. "After the past few days, I'll take

anything I can get free from the Army."

He laughed as he ordered the drink. "That friend of yours," he said. "Romero. Even if he was sure he was dying, it must have taken a lot of nerve for him to pull a stunt like that. Reversing the polarity so that the bird would home in on the beam instead of…"

Anyway, he gave me some technical jargon that sounded like that. I sipped my drink and remembered Wegmann telling me: *We can steer it towards us, or away across the valley.* There hadn't been much time, and Romero had had the tracking instruments downstairs with him. There had been no way for Wegmann, up in the tower, to tell that the great bird of death had turned the wrong way. He would have had no warning until he looked up at the last instant, if he did look up…

"I don't know why they're so hot to learn all about that gizmo, anyway," the young lieutenant said. "After all, it was obsolete. It still worked fine on an old missile like the Wotan, but obviously the new guidance systems had it licked. We haven't had that kind of a malfunction in over a year. I figure that's why Wegmann and the people above him decided to blow the works as spectacularly as they could."

"Just how do you figure that?"

"Why, if it was still good, they'd have kept it a secret, wouldn't they? But they saw we were getting ahead of their interceptor devices, so they decided to get themselves some hot scary publicity while there were still a few missiles flying around that they could work on. At least that's the way I see it… Well, excuse me, sir, there's my target for tonight."

I hadn't known that corny old wartime phrase was still being used, or did he think he was originating a new and bright turn of speech that would take the country by storm? He was young enough, and I watched him go to meet a girl who was just as young, in very high heels and a short wide dress bouncing on top of a lot of frilly petticoats. When I was a kid, it practically killed a girl to have her slip show, but nowadays girls seem to consider themselves undressed, without a few lingerie ruffles on display.

Well, if they wanted to show off their pretty underwear, that was their business; I was thinking like an old-timer bemoaning the passing of the beautiful bustles and high-button shoes of his youth. I looked at myself in the mirror and didn't like what I saw. Sure, the job had got done, and I suppose that was the main thing, but a guy named LeBaron had died bailing me out of one hole, and a guy named Romero had died bailing me out of another—all I'd done was talk tough and mean and run like hell.

"Hello, darling," she said. "I don't think much of it, either. That face, I mean."

I turned slowly. She was there, all right. The last time I'd seen her, I'd hauled her out of the truck cab looking like a broken and tattered doll that might have cost somebody a lot of money once but wasn't worth much now. You don't ride a half-ton truck down a steep hillside and bump up against a couple of pine stumps without a little damage. Also keep in mind she'd been no vision of immaculate loveliness at the start of the plunge.

I'd left her, I recalled, so I could attend to some business at the rear of the wrecked pickup; then I'd come back and dragged her away... But there was no hint of that in the appearance of the woman who faced me now. She'd had her hair re-done in the loose, fluffy way I remembered, and she was wearing a startling, short, cocktail dress of some velvety material that looked blacker than black. The startling thing about the dress was that it not only had no sleeves, it had no back, either. In front, covered to the throat, she looked almost demure; behind, bare to the waist, she was practically naked.

"That," I said, "is one hell of a garment to spring on the fine old cowtown of Alamogordo."

She smiled. "I know, darling. According to Helm, my taste in clothes is lousy. My pants are too tight, and my dresses are too bare. What are you celebrating, the end of the world? If so, may I join you?"

"Be my guest." I made room for her beside me and got her a drink. Then I frowned belatedly. "My God, is it tonight? I'd forgotten."

She tasted her whiskey and nodded. "At two o'clock. Oh-two-hundred, according to the Army's silly way of telling time. Why they want to shoot it off in the middle of the night, I don't know. But then, I don't know why they do anything they do, including asking questions." She hesitated. "Matt?"

"Yes?"

"What do you think?"

"About what?"

Her eyes narrowed. "Don't be stupid. You know what I mean. Naldi wasn't crazy, and he wasn't faking. We both saw him. Maybe he was wrong, but... maybe he wasn't. Anyway, he believed it." There was a little silence; then she said, "Matt, I'm kind of scared. Let's get out of here. If it should come, crazy as it sounds, I don't want to be in a bar."

"What's better than a bar?" I asked. "I mean, what's the choice?"

"You're being very obtuse, darling. I don't usually have to spell it out for a man. The choice, naturally, is your motel room or mine."

I glanced at her quickly, but she was busy producing a cigarette, tapping it, and leaning forward so I could light it—which I did.

"Matt?"

"Yes?"

"Even if it doesn't happen, we won't know, will we? I mean, it's been a week. He said that might be long enough, remember?"

"Yes," I said. "I remember. Maybe we're safe, this time."

"Maybe." She glanced at me. "Well, we wouldn't be much of a loss, would we? Either of us? I saw you, you know."

"Saw me?"

"Yes, I was pretty badly shaken up, really, and everything was kind of hazy; but I came to for a little when you left me there by the truck and went back to... Was it Injection A or B, darling?"

I said, "B, naturally. The one that leaves no traces. Orders were to make it look like an accident. Your friend Mr. Gunther was pretty mashed up back there. That aluminum canopy wasn't nearly as strong as the steel cab that protected us. But I had to make sure. Fortunately, my suitcase was handy, with the kit."

She said, "You're a horrible person."

"Sure," I said. "A motel room was mentioned. Let's not get too far off the subject."

"Don't rush me, darling," she said. "You're a dreadful cold-blooded, ruthless person, but I had to find you tonight. Do you understand? You're the only person I'd care to be with tonight, whatever happens."

"Sure," I said. "I don't think much of you, either, glamor girl. You're unreliable and treacherous and arrogant and selfish. If you happen to think a man's done you a bad turn, you can't even be trusted tied hand and foot. You're mean and vengeful, and the only reason I love you is that I can't hurt you, and even if I do you've had it coming for years. Besides, I know you'll always get back at me somehow."

She was smiling happily at the end of this recital. "But you do love me, don't you?"

"Hell," I said. "You know I do. I—"

Somebody was tapping me on the shoulder. It was the young lieutenant. "Pardon me, sir," he said politely. "You're wanted on the telephone. You were being paged in the dining room. I thought I'd better tell you."

I sighed. "Sure. It might be some important officer

wanting to know the exact number of stones in that damn church tower."

But it wasn't. It was Mac, calling from Washington. "Deckhoff," he said, "Stanislaus Deckhoff, unlikely though the name may sound."

"Well, it doesn't really matter now," I said. I'd asked him to run a make on Wegmann, giving him what I knew.

"The agency responsible for the file wants to know if the card should be removed to inactive."

"I'd say so," I said, "but you'd better warn them they'll never get a firm post-mortem identification. Wegmann-Deckhoff and some other guys and a church and some other buildings are scattered all over the side of a mountain. But, yes, I guess it's safe to call him inactive."

"How is the local situation?" he asked.

"Tapering off," I said.

"If I clear you with the authorities, is there any reason you can't start for Washington at once?"

"Yes, sir," I said. "One. She's waiting in the bar."

He was human after all. He said, "Very well, make it tomorrow morning."

I went back to Gail. In the morning, the world was still there, unchanged. Well, almost unchanged.

ABOUT THE AUTHOR

Donald Hamilton was the creator of secret agent Matt Helm, star of 27 novels that have sold more than 20 million copies worldwide.

Born in Sweden, he emigrated to the United States and studied at the University of Chicago. During the Second World War he served in the United States Naval Reserve, and in 1941 he married Kathleen Stick, with whom he had four children.

The first Matt Helm book, *Death of a Citizen*, was published in 1960 to great acclaim, and four of the subsequent novels were made into motion pictures starring Dean Martin in the title role. A new Matt Helm movie is currently in pre-production at Steven Spielberg's Dreamworks studio. Hamilton was also the author of several outstanding stand-alone thrillers and westerns, including two novels adapted for the big screen as *The Big Country* and *The Violent Men*.

Donald Hamilton died in 2006.